HAMSTER-SAURUS REX

VS. THE CUTE-POCALYPSE

BY TOM O'DONNELL

ILLUSTRATED BY TIM MILLER

HAMSTER-SAURUS REX

S.
THE CUTE-
POCALYPSE
HARPER
An Imprint of HarperCollinsPublishers

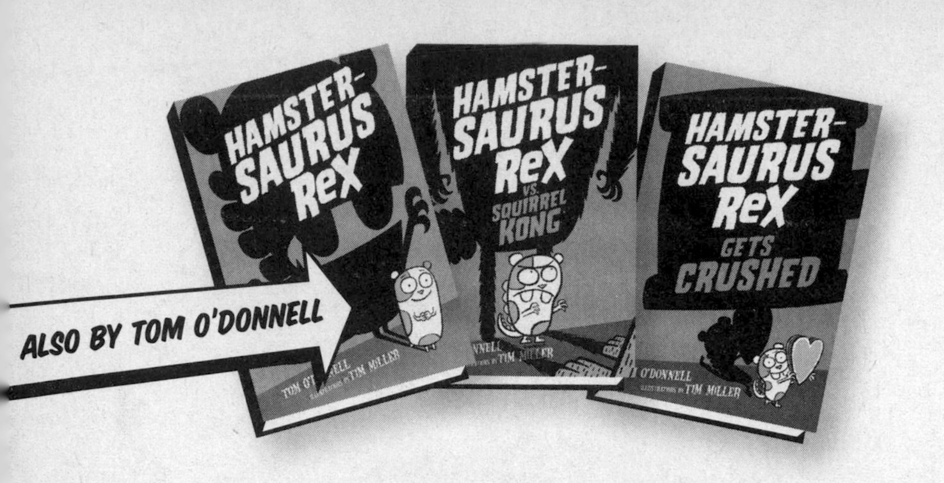

Also by Tom O'Donnell

Hamstersaurus Rex

Hamstersaurus Rex vs. Squirrel Kong

Hamstersaurus Rex Gets Crushed

Hamstersaurus Rex vs. the Cutepocalypse

For information address HarperCollins Children's Books, a division of HarperCollins Publishers, 195 Broadway, New York, NY 10007.
www.harpercollinschildrens.com

ISBN 978-0-06-237760-9

Typography by Joe Merkel
18 19 20 21 22 PC/LSCH 10 9 8 7 6 5 4 3 2 1
❖
First Edition

For my mom and dad
—T.O.D.

For Andrew
—T.M.

CONTENTS

CHAPTER 1

"...AND BY ADDING lobster to your dessert," said Mr. Copeland, "you can really get your money's worth at a cruise-ship buffet."

Seventeen-eighteenths of the class reacted to this pearl of wisdom with bored silence. But Martha Cherie's hand shot up at lightning speed.

"Um, what exactly does this have to do with the Industrial Revolution?" asked Martha.

I'll admit the long digression about stretching your cruise-ship dollar seemed a bit off topic to me, too. But who was I to judge? At that very moment, I was in the middle of drawing

Hamstersaurus Rex battling Hades, the Greek god of the underworld.

"You know, that is a great question, Martha," said Mr. Copeland, throwing his besandaled feet up onto his desk. "And it's one I want you to mull over and ask your seventh-grade teacher on the first day of school next year. Because isn't the most important part of learning sometimes *not knowing the answer?*"

"Not knowing the answer gives me a very pronounced rash," said Martha, scratching her

neck. “And we still have four weeks of class left, Mr. Copeland.”

“Nope,” said Mr. Copeland. “We have three weeks, four days, and eleven minutes of class left. But please, call me Arnold.”

As the end of the school year approached, the mood at Horace Hotwater Middle School had started to change. Everyone was, in a word, preoccupied. Omar Powell began wearing Hawaiian shirts to class every day. Caroline Moody steered all conversations toward her upcoming Grand Canyon vacation. Wilbur Weber was pretty excited for something called “SnailCon.” Jared Kopernik was going to spend his summer searching for the Loch Ness Monster. He was planning to check out the “one place nobody had ever thought to look”: Sheboygan, Wisconsin.

The only thing my best friend, Dylan D’Amato, could talk about was the training camp she would be attending in July, put on by disc golf legend Alfonso "The Wrist" Chapman. She was particularly thrilled because the newest Hotwater Discwhipper, Drew McCoy, would be attending the camp with her.

Martha Cherie also seemed happy about the impending summer break. She was glad to have "conquered" sixth grade and eager to move on to seventh, thereby putting her one small step closer to full adulthood. You'd think that as hard as she worked all year, she'd be looking forward to relaxing. But there would be no unstructured free time for Martha. Summer was her chance to spend all day, every day, doing résumé-building extracurricular activities. She had a slate of externships, clubs, camps, and lessons lined up that are too numerous to list here.

In fact, there was probably only one kid at Horace Hotwater who wasn't looking forward to vacation: me. I don't often admit it, but deep down, I actually kind of like school. My grades may not be great, but I get to draw a lot and I know what I'm having for lunch up to a week in advance. Normally I would spend my summer break hanging out with Dylan, but she would be gone for most of the time. Now I was staring down two and a half solid months of boredom. It's not like I had nothing going on. I was hoping to finish my new movie script called *The Swords of Hamstervalia*—the first installment of a nine-part epic fantasy saga about a faraway kingdom of hamsters that had swords—but so far I hadn't gotten much further than the title. The only bright side of the summer break was that no evil, monolithic corporation would be menacing me.

That's right. SmilesCorp was done. Serena Sandoval's blog post exposé had a bigger effect than anyone could have dreamed. Millions of people had read her account of the company's nefarious mutant-related misdeeds. It even made national news. I don't exactly understand all the corporate ins and outs (Martha tried to explain it all to me once), but thanks to the terrible press, SmilesCorp's stock price had plummeted, forcing the company to declare bankruptcy. A few months back, they permanently closed their Maple Bluffs campus.

That was great news for Hamstersaurus Rex and me, and not-so-great news for the local economy. SmilesCorp was by far the biggest employer in the area. When they closed up shop, all their employees—including my mom—were unceremoniously laid off. Thankfully she quickly found a new job at the municipal library. Others weren't so lucky.

As I finished my drawing, Mr. Copeland elaborated on the importance of putting sunscreen on the tops of your feet so you don't get flip-flop tan lines. Martha sighed, frustrated by the lack of educational content. The final bell rang. This afternoon I had somewhere to be.

"Hey, Dylan," I said, "I think there might be a part for you in *The Swords of Hamstervalia*, once I write it. Could you play a valorous shield-maiden who follows the ancient Hamster Code of Chivalry?"

“Sounds pretty cool,” said Dylan. “But I’m honestly not sure I’ll have the time. It’s going to be a busy summer.”

“No, yeah, me too. My mom wants me to clean out the attic so I’m pretty slammed also,” I said. “Anyway, do you want to walk over to 3223 Birchpoplar Way together?”

“Sounds great,” said Dylan. “We just need a few minutes to swing by our lockers. We’re planning on wearing matching sweaters to the party.”

“We?” I said.

“Me and Drew,” said Dylan. She stared at me like I was insane.

“Really?” I said. “I thought this was a friends-only type deal and I’m not sure Drew is exactly—”

“’Sup,” said Drew McCoy as he sidled over to us.

Dylan laughed loudly.

“. . . Was there a joke in there somewhere that I missed?” I said.

“No, it was more, like, his timing,” said Dylan, still giggling. “‘’Sup.’ Classic. Man, Drew is so funny.”

“Sure,” I said. “Hey, Drew. How’s the stuff

you're . . . um, what are your interests again?"

"I like collecting comic books but not reading them," said Drew, "wearing cool fedoras, and of course, my newest passion is disc golf." He gave me a double thumbs-up.

"Awesome," I said.

"Drew is a real Renaissance man," said Dylan. "You know, he should be in your movie, too! As the main character!"

"Yeaaaaah," I said. "Well, I just remembered I forgot to buy a gift to bring to the party, so maybe I'll probably just meet you guys there."

"I already have a great gift that we could just say is from both of us," said Martha, appearing out of nowhere like some sort of apple-polishing cat burglar. "It's an eight-pack of three-ring binders. Very practical."

"Right. Cool. That's an idea," I said to Martha, who could always trample a good excuse. "But . . . wouldn't that just reward my laziness instead of teaching me a valuable lesson?"

"Good point," said Martha.

"So, instead I'll just swing by Tenth Street Toys

on the way there," I said.

"Toys," said Martha, stroking her jaw. "That's an interesting gift option. I usually just give my friends office supplies. I wish I could go with you, Sam, but I've got to swing by the school office and then I'm having a surprise fifteen-minute Model Interplanetary Council micro-practice before the party."

"Seriously, Martha?!" said Julie Bailey, who I didn't know had been eavesdropping on our conversation. "We had a three-hour macro-practice yesterday!"

"Yes, and you have a lot of room for improvement, Bailey!" said Martha. "You need to focus, because we are in this thing to win it. In Model Interplanetary Council there's no second place. Only first planetary loser!"

"Yikes," I said. "Well, anyway, I've got to run. Later, Martha. Bye, Dylan."

Dylan stared at me.

"Goodbye, Drew," I said with a sigh.

"'Sup," said Drew, as I dashed off.

I made a beeline for the school library, where

the official Horace Hotwater Hamster Habitat now resided. These days Hamstersaurus Rex was no longer confined to a dusty closet filled with unwanted books. He wasn't even locked in a sturdy PETCATRAZ Pro™ (the toughest small rodent cage on the market). He now had the run of an ever-expanding network of interconnected PETCATRAIL Pipes™: clear plastic tubes that supposedly simulated a hamster's natural habitat in the wild (I guess there are a lot of plastic tubes out there in the woods or wherever hamsters live). The PETCATRAIL had already spread to every corner of the library (I'll admit I may have gotten a little carried away when I built the thing).

"Sam, you better not be adding more pipes to this monstrosity," said Mrs. Baxley, the school librarian. "You've already completely blocked off access to the microfilm reader! Someone may want to use it again someday!"

"Sorry, Mrs. Baxley," I said. "I guess we could move the whole setup back to Room 223b. Even though it doesn't get any natural light and

Hamstersaurus Rex *did* save the whole school on multiple occasions. . . ."

"No, no, it's fine," grumbled Mrs. Baxley. "I'll just add 'zookeeper' to my job description. . . ."

"Not zookeeper," I said. "Hamster Monitor. And I'm happy to make you a badge and lanyard if you like."

Mrs. Baxley scowled. I didn't feel too guilty, though. All the extra space wasn't just for Hamstersaurus Rex. Inside the central PETCATRAIL bubble I saw Cartimandua snoring away peacefully on a bed of soft cedar chips.

"Rise and shine, Cartimandua," I said. "Time for the soiree."

Cartimandua yawned and rolled over, which was her version of a friendly greeting. Just then, three tiny shapes came tumbling out of one of the tubes: Stompy, Chompy, and Hatshepsut.

"Heya, kiddos!" I said. "Ready to party?"

The three hamster pups hopped up and down, jostling the cage and squeaking with delight. That's right, a month ago Cartimandua and Hamstersaurus Rex had a litter! Each of the little fuzzballs

JUST ASK!
CHECK IT OUT!

BUMP TIME!
PLATO
CATS

was one-quarter dinosaur and 100 percent adorable. Chompy took after his father in the pointy teeth department. He pretty much tried to eat anything that wasn't nailed down (including, one time, actual nails). Stompy had oversized dinosaur feet and, if I'm being honest, a bit of an anger management issue (kids go through phases, I'm told). Hatshepsut (named by Martha) was totally hyperactive, bouncing off the walls of the enclosure with a perpetually whipping T. rex tail.

Right behind them came their frazzled father. Hamstersaurus Rex's eyes were bloodshot and his fur stood out in greasy clumps. I noticed more than a few new gray hairs among the orange patches.

"Wow, buddy," I said. "You look like you just got

stomped on by Squirrel Kong. Only less rested."

Hatshepsut started wailing. Hamstersaurus Rex sighed and separated her from Chompy, who was gnawing on his sister's tail. Meanwhile Stompy managed to kick the metal hamster wheel hard enough so that it wobbled and almost fell on top of her head. Hamstersaurus Rex gasped and caught it just before it did.

"Hammie, you think you're stressed out now," I said, "wait till they start driving!"

It was a joke I'd heard Dylan's father tell about 150 times. I figured Hamstersaurus Rex would appreciate a dad joke. Instead he just squinted at me. The little guy loved his pups, but total responsibility for three new lives was really stressing him out. He was used to being the maniac, not taking care of maniacs. Cartimandua, as you might guess, was very laid-back about the whole parenthood thing. None of the commotion had woken her up.

I scooped the happy hamster family out of the PETCATRAIL and tucked them into my backpack.

"Chompy, no biting. Stompy, no kicking," I said.

"Hatshepsut, just try not to get overstimulated."

Hamstersaurus Rex gave another weary sigh as I zipped them up. Soon I was jogging down the front steps of Horace Hotwater Middle School. Twenty minutes after that, I was at my neighborhood toy store trying to think of a good gift for Beefer Vanderkoff for his bar mitzvah. If you'd told me eight months ago that I'd be celebrating the day my lifelong bully became a man, I would have countered that you were completely nuts. But then again, I suppose I wouldn't have believed you about the giant squirrel or the evil telepathic mole either. Sixth grade is full of surprises!

"Can I help you, son?" said Mr. Lomax, the owner of Tenth Street Toys. "Or are you just planning to lovingly caress some toys that your mom is never going to buy you?"

I was a bit of a regular here.

"Oh, I'm definitely buying something today," I said. "Don't you worry about that, Mr. Lomax."

"I'll believe it when I see it," said Mr. Lomax. "You didn't bring your weird, scaly hamster in here, did you? Because you know the rule." He pointed to a handwritten sign on the door that read "NO WEIRD, SCALY HAMSTERS."

"*Of course* I know the rule," I said, which was technically a true non-lie answer. This policy had been put in place after an incident in which Hamstersaurus Rex (allegedly) gobbled the whole bowl of free peppermints by the cash register. Personally I didn't see how you could steal something that was free and I doubted the case would hold up in a court of law.

"Because I swear I just saw your backpack move," said Mr. Lomax.

"That is odd," I said. "My backpack is actually full of, uh, regular school items."

"Regular school items?" said Mr. Lomax. His eyes narrowed. "Like what?"

"Well, there's an apple," I said. "To honor my teacher, of course. And a protractor. And a couple of those, uh, graduation caps with the tassel thingies . . ."

His expression softened. "Good boy. Study hard and one day you could own an unprofitable toy store. Now what can I help you with today?"

I breathed a sigh of relief. "Well, I need to get a cool toy for my . . ." I paused and considered my words carefully. "Yeah, all right, fine, I guess he's my *friend*."

"Well, then," said Mr. Lomax, now flashing a smile. "Might I suggest the Gamehouser APEX 720-X3 with Seven-Game Bundle?" He pointed to a video game system on the top shelf behind the counter. The price tag said $499.99.

I swallowed. "You know, he's actually more of an, er, acquaintance," I said. "In fact, he used to stick me in toilets. Any gifts for someone like that?"

Mr. Lomax frowned. "Feel free to browse," he said. "As you well know, the cheapo toys are in aisle four."

That's where I headed. Good old aisle four: where a kid who'd blown his birthday money long ago might still find a little happiness. Could I get away with giving Beefer a set of finger puppets and some wax lips? Nah, that was probably too cheap. He had risked his life to help Hamstersaurus Rex and me in the fight against the evil Mind Mole. What if I threw in some Silly Putty, too?

I wandered into aisle five and continued to rack my brain. Beefer liked snakes, Renaissance music, and stomach-churning horror movies. But had he ever mentioned pogo sticks? What about magnetic chess sets? I started to second-guess myself. If he was becoming a man, should I even be getting him a toy? Maybe what he needed was a flannel bath-robe? Or one of those special spoons for eating grapefruit? Maybe a set of preemptive dentures?

On an otherwise empty shelf near the back, a strange box caught my eye: inside was an adorable, furry toy with pointed, bat-like ears and an antenna poking out of the top of its head. Its large eyes were closed.

I picked the box up. The package said it was a “Snuzzle,” made by a company called Fundai. I’d never heard of them. This particular Snuzzle was named “Gooboo.” According to the text on the back, Snuzzles were “all new” and “oodles of fun.” It promised a fully USB-chargeable electronic “BFF” that could walk, talk, obey simple commands, and even communicate wirelessly with your friends’ Snuzzles “up to one hundred feet away." It was, and I quote, "the ultimate twenty-first-century smartpet experience."

"Check it out, Hammie," I said into my backpack. "You're a pretty good 'smartpet experience' but this thing says it's got you beat—"

Suddenly, the Snuzzle's eyelids popped open.

"Whoa!" I said, dropping the box and stumbling backward into a rack of stuffed armadillos.

"HEWWO," said the Snuzzle, "FWIEND?"

My heart melted. "Awww. Hi there, little fellow," I said. "Aren't you a cutie?"

Hamstersaurus Rex gave a grunt as he peeked his head out of my backpack to see what the hubbub was.

The Snuzzle blinked again. Its eyes had changed from friendly yellow to red.

"DESTWOY," said the Snuzzle. And it burst out of its cardboard packaging and flew right at me.

CHAPTER 2

THUD! THE SNUZZLE head-butted me right in the gut. It knocked the wind out of me and I staggered backward into an RC boat display. Wow. The toy might have been the size of a bread loaf but it had cyborg strength!

"That . . . wasn't . . . oodles of fun," I coughed from under a pile of remote-controlled submarines.

"DESTWOY," said the Snuzzle again, and it crouched for another attack.

With a deafening roar, Hamstersaurus Rex somersaulted out of my backpack and landed between the Snuzzle and me. The little guy was ready to defend me at any cost!

“DESTWOY,” repeated the Snuzzle.

At the same instant, Hamstersaurus Rex and the Snuzzle charged. They smashed into each other with a horrendous crunching clang. The Snuzzle bit down on Hammie’s leg with its mechanical mouth. Meanwhile Hammie clawed at the thing with his back feet, stripping away clumps of fake fur and revealing plastic and metal underneath.

“Mr. Lomax!” I yelled. “I think your Snuzzle might be, um, defective?”

There was no response.

CRASH! Hammie and the Snuzzle, still locked in mortal combat, had toppled the divider between aisle six and aisle seven. Dozens of Debbie Future dolls went flying everywhere. With his powerful dino-jaws, Hammy chomped right through Snuzzle's rubbery left ear. Sparks shot out of the hole in its head. The Snuzzle picked up a die-cast metal fire truck and bashed Hamstersaurus Rex across the face with it, knocking him woozy. Hammie staggered.

I heard a furious squeak from my open backpack. It was Stompy, peeking out, her tiny eyes filled with rage.

"No, Stompy!" I said. "Your dad's got this! Stay in the backpack!"

"DESTWOY," said the Snuzzle as it leaped into the air and landed on Hammie's back. "DESTWOY . . . DESTWOY . . . DESTWOY . . ." It jumped up and down on his limp body, pummeling him into the linoleum. It was starting to look like maybe Hamstersaurus Rex *didn't*, in fact, have this.

"Gooboo, stop!" I yelled. "I . . . voice command you! Leave him alone!"

The Snuzzle paid me no attention. Fine, so much for that feature. On the box it also showed that the Snuzzle had an "on/off" switch hidden under a flap on its back. I ducked in and somehow managed to flick the switch on the first try. Nothing happened. The switch didn't work. What the heck? Meanwhile, the Snuzzle was still using Hamstersaurus Rex as a trampoline.

I looked around for a weapon. Foam pool noodle? No. Plastic samurai sword? No. Pretend pizza cutter? No! Turns out a toy store isn't the easiest place to arm yourself to fight an evil robot. I grabbed my best option—a jumbo plush banana wearing a beret—and swung it with all my strength. The banana blow sent it clattering across the toy store floor. All right!

The Snuzzle was back on its feet in an instant. It picked up a Max Stomper: Arctic Detective action figure and hurled it at me. I just managed to duck, but the toy almost took my head off! The Snuzzle grabbed another Max Stomper.

Just then—*plink*—a tiny shape kicked the Snuzzle from behind. It was Stompy, snarling and baring her teeth in a pretty good impression of her dad. She kicked the Snuzzle again.

Slowly the Snuzzle's head turned 180 degrees with a grinding mechanical creak.

"DESTWOY," it said.

RRRRRROOOOOARRRR! With a terrifying roar that set off several car alarms outside, Hamstersaurus Rex hit the Snuzzle like a freight train. The Snuzzle pinwheeled through the air, ricocheted off a light fixture, and made a faint crashing sound somewhere on the opposite end of the toy store.

"Wow! That was a super dino mega-attack the likes of which I've never seen before!" I said. "Power level unlocked!"

But Hamstersaurus Rex didn't look triumphant or even angry. He looked scared. He clutched Stompy close to him as his eyes darted around, wary of danger.

I ran down the aisle to see what had happened to the Snuzzle. From what I could tell, it had flown all the way to the front near the register and . . .

"Oh no," I said.

The Gamehouser APEX 720-X3 with Seven-Game

Bundle box had been flattened like an accordion by the impact. But where was the Snuzzle?

Slowly, I peered over the counter. Lying in a pile of dust and loose toys on the floor was Gooboo. After the battle, the cute little creature was quite a gruesome sight: half its face had been ripped off, exposing the bare metal beneath. Smoke curled from its empty left eye socket. The eye itself was dangling from a few wires. The Snuzzle wasn't moving.

"I was in the bathroom for *five minutes*!"

I turned to see Mr. Lomax. His mouth was hanging open. There were dolls and action figures everywhere, toppled aisles, and broken display racks.

"Mr. Lomax!" I said. "A toy went nuts and tried to kill us!"

"Us?" said Mr. Lomax.

"Me and Ham— Doesn't matter," I said. "Anyway, it's right here. It's called a Snuzzle!"

"Snuzzle?" said Mr. Lomax. "Impossible!"

"Please!" I cried. "Just look!" I pointed behind the counter right to where the Snuzzle wasn't.

Mr. Lomax moaned as he took in more of the destruction. "You turned that Gamehouser APEX 720-X3 with Seven-Game Bundle into a piece of modern art," he said, burying his face in his hands. "And not the kind I like, with the soup cans!"

"Wait. No," I said, looking around desperately. "The Snuzzle's got to be here."

From the corner of my eye, I saw the store's front door swing closed as if someone or something had just exited.

"There!" I cried. "Gooboo is getting away!" I started to run but Mr. Lomax caught me by the sleeve.

"Oh no you don't, son," said Mr. Lomax. "You're

not going anywhere. A crime has been committed here."

"What?" I said. "But I didn't do this. That Snuzzle has a major malfunction. On the box it should say 'Ages *Never* and Up'!"

"Maybe technically you didn't do this," said Mr. Lomax. "But your weird little hamsters did!"

He pointed down at what was left of aisle seven. There stood Hamstersaurus Rex, with Stompy, Chompy, Hatshepsut, and Cartimandua behind him.

"I see you've raised an army of them now, bent on my destruction!" he said. "Revenge for telling you not to steal mints!"

"Okay, that's a tad dramatic," I said. "Don't you have security cameras or something? Can we just go to the tape?"

Once Mr. Lomax was confident that my "army of evil hamsters" were properly restrained (i.e., back in my backpack), we did go to the tape. The store security cameras were linked to the old computer Mr. Lomax had by the register. But thanks to the ancient system—with its grainy low-res cameras pointed at odd angles—the video simply looked like Hamstersaurus Rex trashed the place for no reason.

"This footage is terrible," I said. "My UltraLite SmartShot can record at twice the resolution of these antiques you're using—"

"First you smash up my store, then you insult my security cameras! Such disrespect," said Mr. Lomax, shaking his head. "Son, I am now going to call the appropriate authorities, and you and your hamster vandal gang will face the full judgment of the law." He reached for the phone on his desk.

"Wait!" I said. It was bad enough when Hamstersaurus Rex had to tangle with Maple Bluffs Animal Control, but I had no desire for the real police to get involved. "Mr. Lomax, I promise I'll make this right!"

He paused.

"I'll help you clean up the store," I said. "See, look at this." I picked up a stuffed armadillo and put it back on the rack.

"Oh wow, thanks so much, Mr. Good Samaritan," said Mr. Lomax. "But that's not enough. Look at all the stuff your attack hamster broke." Mr. Lomax gestured to the toy carnage. "I can't run an unprofitable toy store when all my inventory has been destroyed."

"Well, maybe I could pay you back . . . somehow," I said. "Like maybe I could work here part-time, after school?"

"You think I want to spend *more* time with you?" said Mr. Lomax. "Read the room, son!"

I winced. "Then I'll just get you the money. But the thing is . . . I kind of blew my birthday cash two weeks ago. On an oversized slingshot."

"Did you purchase it here?" said Mr. Lomax. He pointed to a whole aisle of oversized slingshots.

"No," I said quietly. "Online."

"The indignities never end," said Mr. Lomax, shaking his head.

"In my defense, it was three dollars cheaper," I mumbled.

"That's it," said Mr. Lomax. "You obviously have no conscience, and now I really am calling the cops!" He grabbed the phone and started to dial. "Enjoy jail!"

"I'll pay you back," I cried. "I promise!"

He slowly put the receiver back down. "You have two weeks," said Mr. Lomax. "And I want it in writing." He pushed a pad of paper and a pen in my direction.

I sighed and wrote out the following sentence, as dictated by Mr. Lomax: "I, Sam Gibbs, promise to pay Tenth Street Toys back for all the toys that got broken." I signed it and handed it back to him. It wasn't fair. But when you're a kid, turns out a lot of things aren't.

"Okay then," said Mr. Lomax. "That three dollars you saved by not supporting local businesses can be your first down payment on the $627.14 you owe me." He held out his hand.

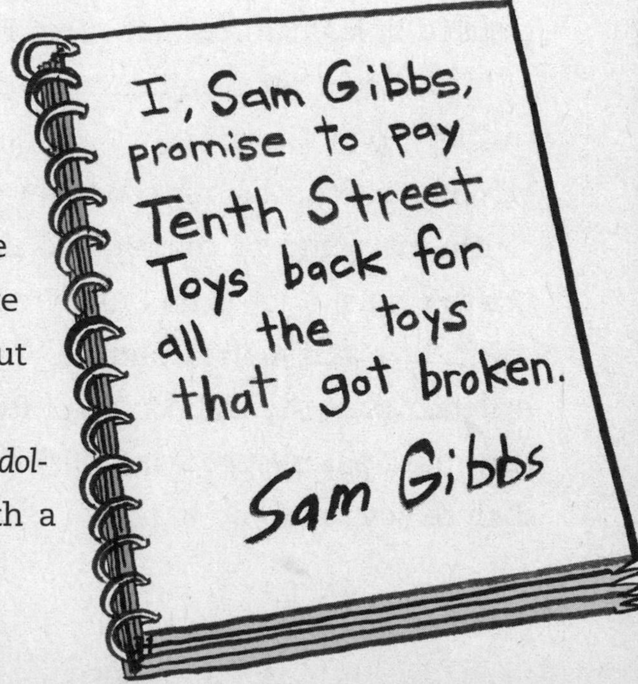

"*Six hundred dollars?*" I said with a

gasp. I felt like I might throw up, or faint, or both, a couple of times.

"No. Not six hundred dollars," said Mr. Lomax. "Six hundred twenty-seven dollars and fourteen cents: $499.99 for the Gamehouser APEX 720-X3 with Seven-Game Bundle, $55.56 for the eight broken Debbie Future dolls, $61.98 for the two smashed Bathtime Blitzers RC Submarines with Realistic Periscope Action, and last but not least, $9.61 for the Max Stomper: Arctic Detective action figure that you somehow managed to embed in the ceiling!"

He pointed up. Sure enough, Max Stomper's muscular legs protruded from a hole above us.

"Oh," said Mr. Lomax. "And one fifty for the mints."

"But there's no realistic way I can come up with that kind of money," I said. "I'm a child. I don't have a job. The only time I get money is birthdays and major holidays. And even if it *was* my birthday, I usually only get forty dollars from my grandparents. At that rate, I'll be twenty-eight before I can pay you back."

"Interesting," said Mr. Lomax. "This contract you just signed says you have two weeks. Now let's see that three bucks, kid."

I reached into my pocket and started counting out coins. . . .

"And that's when I gave him $2.89 in change," I said.

"Awesome," said Dylan.

Hamstersaurus Rex squinted at her.

"How is that awesome?" I said. "Were you even listening?"

"Huh? No," said Dylan. "I was talking about Drew's sweater. I think it's awesome. And also totally rad."

I gritted my teeth. "Those are synonyms."

Indeed, Dylan and Drew McCoy had changed into their matching sweaters before the party as promised. They were yellow with little turquoise whales all over them.

"Ever wonder who came up with sleeves?" said Drew, ignoring me as he admired his own. "I bet they're superrich."

Dylan nodded.

I tried not to make a face. "Anyway, guys, long story short: I apparently owe Tenth Street Toys over six hundred dollars and there's also a deadly malfunctioning toy on the loose. So much for closing out sixth grade without any more drama."

"It's a tragedy," said Martha.

"Thank you," I said. "Finally, a little sympathy."

"I'm not talking about you fighting the Snuzzle," said Martha. "I'm talking about this." She held up a sheet of paper full of numbers in columns. "I swung by the office to give Principal Truitt her birthday card—"

"Of course," said Dylan.

"—and I learned my official grade point average is 3.99."

"Okay," I said, confused. "That's . . . good?"

"No, it isn't!" said Martha.

"It isn't?" I said. "Well, who cares?"

"I cares!" said Martha. She suddenly cupped both hands over her mouth. "For the first time in my life I just made a grammatical mistake. Oh no. Everything I've worked for, it's starting to spiral out of control."

“Martha, how could you possibly have less than 4.0?” said Dylan. “Grades are like your disc golf.”

“I don’t know!” said Martha, grabbing Dylan by the sweater. “It must be a clerical error. But I’ve already talked to Principal Truitt, and the superintendent, and the governor’s office, and *nobody can give me a straight answer*!”

“Calm down,” I said. “Don’t they just toss out all our middle school grades when we go to high school anyway?”

Martha glared at me. “How dare you, Sam,” she said. “How *dare* you.”

“Look, I see that you’re pretty upset,” I said, “but just to reiterate: a fuzzy superstrong cyborg literally tried to murder me.”

“Sounds like it could be huge,” said Serena Sandoval, who was twirling a lock of her now-green hair while she checked her phone. After her article blew up, she persuaded her dad to get her one. Now she was always checking it.

"That's what I'm trying to tell you guys!" I said.

"Sam, do you think a blog post about this could be described as 'shareable content'?" said Serena, now taking notes in her notes app.

"Uh. I don't know," I said. "Maybe? Yeah, maybe you could use your blog to, like, help investigate! I know you've been looking to do a follow-up to the SmilesCorp story and it's been a few—"

"*I know how long it's been!*" said Serena, with a touch of panic in her voice. "I'm pursuing a number of angles. Running down various leads. Journalism takes time. Things are really coming together. Anyway, what I need is a story that really engages the reader, and people like to share videos. Is there video?"

"Well, the quality of the store's security footage was bad," I said. "You couldn't tell what was going on. All choppy and pixelated."

"Hmm," said Serena. "No video. Not great. Maybe we could get by on the strength of a snappy yet slightly misleading headline?"

"What do you mean?" I said.

"This Little Boy Walked into a Toy Store Hoping

for a Miracle. You'll Never Believe What Happened Next," said Serena.

"I wasn't hoping for a miracle," I said. "And I'm not—I'm *slightly* shorter than the average American male sixth grader. You can check the stats on that!"

"You're a shrimp," said Beefer, walking toward us in his rumpled oversized suit. He stuffed a piece of cake into his mouth.

"Beefer, it's your special day," I said, gritting my teeth. "So I'm not going to hit you with a sick comeback about which sea creature you happen to resemble. Mazel tov, buddy."

"Probably an awesome shark with sunglasses on," said Beefer, shoveling more cake into his mouth. The ceremonial part of the bar mitzvah was over and now it was time for the party. The only problem: Dylan, Martha, Serena, Drew, and I were the only ones who showed up! It was a pretty grim celebration. Beefer scanned his empty backyard, festooned with decorations, DJ blaring music. His eyes fell on Drew. "So who invited this guy?"

"I did," said Dylan, crossing her arms. "And right now he's making up sixteen percent of your total guests. So be nice."

"'Sup?" said Drew.

"Dude, I feel like I know you," said Beefer.

"Yeah. We went to school together for five and a half years," said Drew.

"Is your name . . . Marcus?" said Beefer.

"No," said Drew.

Beefer shrugged. "Agree to disagree," he said. "Thank you for coming, Martha. It was very *infusible* of you, m'lady."

"You're welcome, Beefer," said Martha, still scowling at her transcript. "I wish I could have fun, but I'm too busy fretting."

"Cool, cool," said Beefer.

"You mind if I film this party for a blog post about sad parties?" asked Serena. She started shooting video of a partially deflated balloon on her smartphone.

"Don't do that!" said Beefer. "Things are really going to pick up when my friend Tony gets here. And he's going to bring his friend . . . Tony! You'll see! They're real!"

"Wow," said Serena, filming him. "That was really poignant."

"Sam, can I talk to you for a second?" said Beefer, under his breath.

"Actually," I said, "I was about to check out that make-your-own-taco station—"

"Sam needs to go to the bathroom. Very urgent," said Beefer, grabbing me by the elbow and yanking me to my feet. "We'll be back soon. You guys continue to have the greatest time of your lives."

Martha was still frowning at her grades. Dylan and Drew were admiring each other's sweaters. Serena was checking her phone.

Beefer pulled me behind a large boxwood bush. "Sam, this party is a flop and it's all your fault," he said.

"What?" I said. "How could this possibly be my fault?"

"I don't know!" said Beefer. "That's just kind of my go-to when something bad happens! How come I don't have any friends?"

"You have . . . your pet boakeet," I said.

"Michael Perkins is the greatest and most loyal companion a guy could ask for and he makes your weird gerbil look like a real dud. No offense," said Beefer. "But I'm talking about *human* friends."

"I don't know, man," I said. "Maybe because most of your life you've been a violent goon?"

"Am not a goon! I'll smash you!" said Beefer, and he slugged me in the arm.

"Ow," I said.

"Sorry, my reflexes kicked in," said Beefer. "Please, Sam, you have to help me. I can't bear having another bar mitzvah where nobody shows up."

"Wait, don't you only get the one?" I said.

"Do I?" said Beefer. He waved his fists at the sky and started to wail: "Oh nooooooo!"

"Look," I said. "I don't even know what you want from me."

"I need you to tell me how to be popular like you," said Beefer. "And since you very rudely didn't bring me a gift, you owe me this."

"Ugh," I said. "First, I didn't get you a gift because an evil toy attacked me!"

"Yeah right," said Beefer. "I've used that excuse a million times."

"Second," I said, "I'm not popular."

"But you are!" said Beefer, as he pointed to where the others were sitting. "Look at them. They're all your friends. They only came here because of you. Even Martha. Literally no one else wanted to come to my party."

"Well, they're *supposedly* my friends," I said. "But they're so preoccupied with their own problems, they won't even listen when I tried to tell them about how I almost got killed on the way here—"

"Sam, please stop talking about yourself!" said Beefer. "This is my special day!"

"Okay, fine," I said. "Well, if you want people to like you, why don't you just, you know, try to be a little nicer?"

"I am too nice! I'll smash you!" said Beefer, and he slugged me in the arm again.

"Ouch!" I said. "That's exactly what I'm talking about."

"Point taken," said Beefer. "So should I hit people less or, like, never?"

Before I could answer, a bloodcurdling shriek came from inside Beefer's house.

CHAPTER 3

HAMSTERSAURUS REX, BEEFER, and I burst into the Vanderkoff house to find a scene of total chaos. There was an upset hors d'oeuvres tray, two overturned cheese plates, and the contents of a chip bowl had been spread across the floor. All the cushions had been thrown off the couch, and a fancy Victorian lamp had been tipped over onto its side.

"It's Gooboo the Snuzzle!" I said.

"Now you're just making up words," said Beefer.

There was another scream from the kitchen.

"That's my mom!" said Beefer. "Mommy, are you okay?"

Just then, the door to the kitchen swung open and something came wriggling out that looked like an eight-foot blue tube sock. It was Michael Perkins, Beefer's pet boa constrictor that had been genetically hybridized with a parakeet. He had a look of sheer terror in his eyes as he slithered and flapped across the floor, toppling an ottoman and knocking all the coasters off the coffee table. Right behind him came three bouncing fuzzballs, no bigger than Mint-Caramel Choconobs. It was Stompy, Chompy, and Hatshepsut, hot on the boakeet's tail. They squeaked with delight as they continued to chase him around the room.

"Guys, come on!" I said. "Please don't roughhouse inside the Vanderkoff residence! You're going to break—"

CRASH! Hatshepsut knocked a teakettle, almost certainly an antique, off an end table and it shattered.

A moment later, Mrs. Vanderkoff came into the room. She had a tight, forced smile on her face. "Hello again, Jarmo," she said through clenched teeth.

"Uh, I actually go by Sam now, ma'am," I said.

"Are these your baby hamsters, Sam?" asked Mrs. Vanderkoff. "Because I must admit, they gave me quite a fright when they chased Kiefer's pet snake through the kitchen; then they ate an entire pan of brownies that was cooling on the counter and ruined a bowl of my famous jalapeño hummus dip in a way that I'd . . . prefer not to describe."

"I'm really, really sorry about that, Mrs. Vanderkoff," I said. "If there's any way I can make it up to you—"

"What? No jalapeño hummus dip? My bar mitzvah is ruined!" cried Beefer. "This is the worst day of my life!" He stomped off and ran upstairs.

I stared at my feet. "You know what, it's actually getting kind of late," I said. "I should probably get going. . . ."

"We hate to see you go, dear," said Mrs. Vanderkoff, in a tone that suggested quite the opposite. "But please don't forget your other one."

She pointed to the armchair in the corner

where Cartimandua was fast asleep. I gathered my hamsters up and beat a hasty retreat.

I got to school early the next morning feeling out of sorts. My gut was still sore where the crazed Snuzzle smashed into me. Even worse, it was troubling to think the broken toy was still out there somewhere. Who would it attack next? And what if they didn't have a pet dino-hamster to defend them? Before the first bell, I returned the whole hamster family to their library habitat and made my way to the lockers.

". . . I'm getting Weebo!" said Omar Powell. "Apparently you can teach her to say 'Pawty on.'"

"I like the look of Gooboo myself," said Jimmy Choi.

I stopped dead in my tracks. "Wait," I said. "Did you just say 'Gooboo'?"

"Uh, eavesdropping much?" said Jimmy, folding his arms.

"Are you talking about the Snuzzle?" I said.

"Of course! What else would I be talking about?"

said Jimmy. "Haven't you already preordered yours?"

"No!" I cried. "You have to cancel that preorder, Jimmy! Last night, a Snuzzle tried to kill me!" I pulled up my shirt to reveal the purple bruise on my stomach.

"Blech," said Jimmy, turning away. "I don't want to see that!"

"Great," said Omar, shaking his head. "Sam is going to make this into a whole big thing."

"It's sad, really," said Caroline Moody, "the way he keeps doing this."

"I'm telling you, they are deadly!" I said.

"They're not deadly," said Caroline. "They're the ultimate twenty-first-century smartpet experience and also oodles of fun! Read the promotional material sometime."

"Don't tell me you ordered one, too!" I said.

"Obviously," said Caroline Moody. "No way am I going to the Grand Canyon without a Snuzzle to play with. I mean, it's basically just a big hole in the ground, right?"

"We all ordered them, Sam," said Omar. "Snuzzles are the hottest toy of the spring season."

"Bigger than Flubjubs and Zingo Spinners combined," said Jimmy.

"And after I get mine," said Omar, with a dreamy look on his face, "I'm pretty sure my life is going to be complete."

I felt like I couldn't breathe. For the first time it dawned on me that the Snuzzle that attacked me wasn't the only one. Of course they were mass-produced. There were thousands of them out there. And if they were all as defective as the one I saw, this was going to be a disaster.

"Hang on," I said. "You mean they haven't been released yet?"

"They go on sale at midnight tomorrow," said Jimmy, checking his watch to be sure.

"But I saw one on the shelves at Tenth Street Toys," I said.

"You did not," said Jimmy.

Caroline Moody gasped. "Was it Oobie?" she said. "I need to buy it!"

"I think you missed the second part," I said. "The Snuzzle head-butted me with robo-strength. If Hamstersaurus Rex hadn't jumped into the mix,

I don't know what would have happened."

"No offense, but this just sounds like another one of your crazy stories," said Omar. "Just like 'Squirrel Kong' and the 'Mind Mole.'"

"But those stories were true!" I cried.

"Exactly," said Omar. "So what are the odds you go three for three?"

"Pretty slim," said Jimmy. Caroline nodded.

Try as I might, I couldn't dissuade them. They were determined to buy their shiny new Snuzzles and I had to do something. Unfortunately, I had no idea what.

I was considering this question as I walked down the hallway, when I noticed two new kids—a boy and a girl who had to be brother and sister. The boy was unsuccessfully trying to operate the water fountain, while the girl clutched a beat-up laptop and looked around suspiciously.

"You really have to stomp the pedal," I said, demonstrating. A spurt of water shot out.

"Thanks!" said the boy, then took a drink.

"You know, this water fountain hasn't really been the same since it was knocked off the wall

by a giant, rampaging squirr—" I stopped myself. "Actually, you two are new here. I don't want to scare you. This is a fine school. Very safe."

"Hey, you wouldn't happen to know how to get to Ms. Alvarez's fifth-grade classroom, would you?" said the boy. "I promised my dad I'd help my sister find her teacher."

"I don't need your help," said the girl, and she rolled her eyes. "I'm not a baby."

"No problem," I said. "Ms. Alvarez's room is on the second floor, beside the bulletin board about bees."

"Since you seem like an experienced classroom guide," said the boy, "you wouldn't be able to help me find Mr. Copeland's classroom, would you?"

"Sure," I said. "It's the second door on the right. He's the guy in the sandals who looks like he stopped caring about a week and a half ago."

The boy gave a loud chuckle, which startled the girl. It startled me, too. I wasn't used to my jokes landing. Very disconcerting.

"Are you transfer students?" I said.

"Yep," said the boy. "My name is Cid Wilkins. This is my little sister, Sarah-Anne."

"It's just Sarah now!" said the girl. "I told you that! Pay attention!"

"Sorry," said Cid. He looked at me and gave an apologetic shrug.

"Transferring in with only a month left in the school year," I said. "That's rough."

"It's fine. Who needs friends anyway?" said Sarah. "Nice to meet you or whatever. Bye." She gave a sigh and walked off, staring at the floor.

"The kid's taking the move kind of hard," said

Cid. "Me, I couldn't be happier to be here at Horace Hotwater Middle School."

"Did you hear about our famous cafeteria mashed potatoes?" I said. "They're even chalkier than their reputation."

"That sounds great," said Cid. "But I'm psyched because this place is the home of Hamstersaurus Rex! Man, I was hoping this was the water fountain that Squirrel Kong smashed." He pulled out an expensive-looking phone and took a quick selfie with the large dent in the side of the fountain.

"So . . . you're a fan of Hamstersaurus Rex?" I said.

"Oh yeah, I read that crazy blog post that was making the rounds a few months ago," said Cid. "Hamstersaurus Rex is, like, my hero." Cid glanced around and lowered his voice. "Have you ever seen the little guy around?"

"From time to time," I said, grinning despite myself.

"Well, where is he?" said Cid, looking around. "Does he have a secret lair? Or, like, an office somewhere? Can I get an appointment?"

I couldn't help it. I liked this kid. "He lives in the library," I said. "Hamstersaurus Rex and I are actually pals."

"Wait," said Cid. "You're not— Are you Sam Gibbs?"

"Yes?" I said.

"Not *the* Sam Gibbs?" said Cid.

"Well, if you do a web search there's an orthodontist in Maryland of the same name who gets more hits," I said. "But I'm the only one here at HHMS."

"Dude, it's so awesome to meet you!" said Cid, shaking my hand. "Can I show you something?"

"Sure," I said.

"From the blog post I know you're a really talented artist," he said. "So I was hoping maybe you could tell me if this is any good or not?"

He reached into his backpack and pulled out a sheet of notebook paper and handed it to me. It was an amazingly detailed drawing of Hamstersaurus Rex battling a giant squid. Hammie Rex practically leaped off the page and the squid's tentacles were rendered with exquisite crosshatching.

I gulped. Cid was way better at drawing than I was.

"Not bad," I said. "If you keep practicing, maybe one day you could— Aw, who am I kidding? They should toss the *Mona Lisa* in the garbage because this is the single greatest artwork of all time!"

Cid laughed again.

That day I showed Cid Wilkins the ropes at Horace Hotwater. I pointed out the desks where Mr. Copeland couldn't see you doodling (back right; back left). During history Cid produced an amazing scene of Hammie Rex smashing through a submarine with his face. After that, I knew I had to bring him to the library to meet Hamstersaurus Rex in person. The little guy took a liking to him instantly.

"Man, Hamstersaurus Rex is like the coolest pet ever!" said Cid, as Hamstersaurus Rex did laps around the top of his head. "I can't believe I'm actually playing with the world's only mutant dinosaur-hamster hybrid!"

"Well, he's not the only one anymore," I said. "He's got a family now."

"What? A family?" said Cid. "That's a totally unexpected twist!"

Stompy, Chompy, and Hatshepsut came bouncing out of the PETCATRAIL Pipes™ and into my open palms. I handed the three hyper hamster pups to Cid, who was ecstatic. They liked him as much as Hammie did (Chompy even gave him a little love chomp). When it was time for lunch, Cid didn't want to leave. But Mrs. Baxley shooed us along.

Cid and I went through the cafeteria line

together and sat down beside Dylan.

"Hi, Dylan," I said. "This is Cid Wilkins. He's new here."

"Nice to meet you," said Cid.

"Um, that's actually Drew's seat," said Dylan, pointing to the one Cid had taken.

"Weird. I don't see his name on it," I said.

"That's just the seat he likes best," said Dylan, with a shrug.

"Can't Drew sit somewhere else?" I said. "Like maybe at a different table? Or perhaps even in a different building? Or country?"

Before Dylan could say anything, Cid moved his tray.

"No problem," said Cid. "I'm new here so I don't have a favorite seat. They're all the same to me."

Drew McCoy sat down at the newly vacant seat. "'Sup," he said. "Anybody else digging how chalky the mashed potatoes are?"

Later in the day, I found out that Cid even liked filming his own movies, too. He had a lot of helpful ideas for *The Swords of Hamstervalia*. He said maybe I shouldn't just *tell* the audience the hamsters had swords. I needed to *show* them they had swords. I'd never thought of it that way. Later, I taught him how to keep Coach Weekes talking so you wouldn't have to play kickball (just ask what "success" means to him!).

Aside from the slight awkwardness with Dylan at lunch, it was a pretty fun school day. After the final bell rang, I waited on the curb outside for my mom to pick me up. Despite the cloudy sky, I was feeling pretty good. A new kid who laughed at my jokes and shared my interests? It suddenly dawned on me that I might have actually made a friend. Maybe Cid and I could hang out this summer and draw stuff and make movies, while everybody else was doing their thing? Nah, he was so cool he wouldn't want to hang out with me. He was probably just being polite.

I was lost in thought when I heard a rustling in the bushes nearby.

"Hello?" I said.

No answer. I looked around. My mom was running a little late and the other after-school stragglers had already gone home. I was alone on an empty stretch of sidewalk in front of Horace Hotwater.

"Is anyone there?" I said. "Jared? Is that you? I'm telling you, man, there aren't any baby bigfoots in the azalea bushes."

Silence. I breathed a sigh of relief.

Then perhaps it was the wind, or maybe a bird, but I would almost swear I heard a single faint word: "DESTWOY." I took a step backward.

The Snuzzle? Was it hunting me?

"Hop in, Bunnybutt!"

I nearly hopped out of my skin as my mom pulled up behind me on the curb. "Sorry I'm late. I got caught behind Old Man Ohlman in the grocery store. He had a folder of coupons from the mid-seventies."

"Mom, I think there's something in the bushes," I said.

"Ah," she said. "Well, I'm sure it'll be there tomorrow."

"Yeah, that's exactly what I'm afraid of," I said. I cocked my head and listened carefully. I heard nothing, just the quiet breeze in the leaves of the trees nearby and the faint sound of kids playing somewhere.

"Come on, son," said my mom. "The tuna fish I bought isn't going to casserole itself."

At last I got into the car. I wasn't about to go poking around in the underbrush for a dangerous, rogue Snuzzle. Especially not without Hamstersaurus Rex by my side. As we drove off, I turned and scanned the bushes behind me. Nothing but shadows.

CHAPTER 4

IF THE SNUZZLE had somehow followed me to school, the attack wasn't just a random malfunction. I'd been targeted. I did some web research on the company that manufactured the toys. Fundai apparently had its headquarters in Japan, where children had been playing with Snuzzles for two years already. From what I could find, there were no reported incidents of them attacking anyone. I called the customer service number on the company's website but the automatic phone tree was all in Japanese. Eventually I gave up. I also tried searching on truthblasters .com but there wasn't anything about a rogue toy terrorizing Maple Bluffs. Instead the boards were abuzz with some sort of "invisible" creature making mischief at the local flea market. Odd, but the Snuzzle that tried to kill me was definitely visible.

The next day at school, I touched base with my friends to see if they had any more luck looking into the matter.

"Yes," said Martha. "I think I've finally gotten to the bottom of it!"

"Really?" I said.

"It seems like in third grade my average in math was coded incorrectly," said Martha. "Thanks to a typo on Ms. Bartholomew's part, the decimal point was in the wrong place, so instead of a 4.0 it was inputted as a 40.0, which the system rejected. Thus the class was erroneously marked incomplete, which has subsequently destroyed my GPA—"

"Martha, I am not talking about your grades!" I said. "There's an evil robot on the loose! My gut is telling me SmilesCorp must have something to do with it."

"SmilesCorp shut down," said Dylan, who was

absentmindedly drawing hearts in her disc golf playbook.

"Oh, really? I hadn't heard!" I said with a bit too much sarcasm in my voice.

Dylan frowned. "Sam, I'm starting to think maybe you actually liked having SmilesCorp after you?" she said. "Now that you're no longer being threatened on a daily basis, you aren't the center of attention anymore. That must really bother you, huh?"

"Nope, doesn't bother me," I said. "Sure, I thought you guys both took the Hamster Monitor oath seriously, but I guess there are more important things in this world. Martha, by all means focus on sorting out this grave .01 grade point average injustice. And Dylan, you can concentrate on picking out more matching sweaters you and Drew can wear to the disc golf camp run by that used car salesman."

"First, I would never wear a sweater to play disc golf. Second, Alfonso 'The Wrist' Chapman led the Pan-American League in scoring for seven seasons in a row," said Dylan. "And his pre-owned automotive dealership has consistently been among the highest performing in the state so that's nothing to be ashamed of either!"

"It's fine," I said. "I still have one friend who's actually interested in helping me get to the bottom of this Snuzzle thing. So I'll see you two later."

"I can't believe she put the decimal point in the wrong place," said Martha, still staring at her transcript. "I wish I could give a math grade to Ms. Bartholomew. . . ."

After school, I took Stompy, Chompy, Hatshepsut, and Cartimandua out of the PETCATRAIL Pipes™ and put them back into the old PETCATRAZ Pro™. They seemed confused as the door clanked shut and I locked it with my official Hamster Monitor key.

"Sorry, little dudes," I said. "It's for your own safety."

Hamstersaurus Rex was worried. But I could tell the little guy was dead set on getting to the bottom of the rogue Snuzzle mystery. The two of us met up with Serena at the Flipburger near her apartment. I ordered a Lil' Cheez for myself, and six Double Flipsos with extra barbecue sauce and a small milk shake for Hammie Rex. Then we got down to business.

"No worries, Sam. I'm a professional," said Serena. "I looked into it."

"Really?" I said. "Thank you so much!"

"First things first, SmilesCorp isn't gone," said Serena, with a gleam in her eye.

"I knew it!" I said, pounding the booth table with my fist so hard it sent a few barbecue sauce packets flying.

"After SmilesCorp went bankrupt, it was purchased by a company that makes organic lip balm," said Serena. "It is now wholly owned by Pappy's Beeswax of Maine."

She held up a small plastic tube. It had a picture of an old lobster fisherman on it, whose skin looked extremely moisturized.

"That . . . doesn't seem very threatening," I said.

"Nope," said Serena. "Unless you're a big fan of chapped lips."

"I'm not," I said. "So what about Fundai, the

company that manufactures the Snuzzles? It's got to be connected somehow, like, in a big shadowy web of corporate intrigue."

"Nope. No connection to SmilesCorp whatsoever," said Serena. "As far as I can tell, they've been around for seventy years in Japan. Makers of the original Astro-Robo toy line."

I sighed. "Well then, it seems like we've just got to keep digging."

Serena bit her lip. "About that," she said. "You see, I'm not sure I can devote any more, ah, *investigative resources* to this story."

"What?" I said.

"I mean, sure, if you find hard evidence of this evil Snuzzle, or better yet HD video, I'm all in," said Serena. "But otherwise, I kind of need to focus on whatever my follow-up to the SmilesCorp blockbuster is going to be. Once you've gone viral, the pressure is unbelievable, Sam. You have no idea."

"You can't be serious," I said.

"I'm trying to run a journalism outlet in the digital age," said Serena with a shrug.

"Journalism outlet?" I said. "It's just your

personal blog and it only has one post up!"

"Don't remind me!" said Serena. "Look, you know who seems like he's got a lot of time on his hands? Beefer! Maybe Beefer could help you figure out this mystery?"

"You realize you just said 'Beefer' and 'figure out' in the same sentence, right?" I said.

She gave another shrug. I handed the rest of my Lil' Cheez to Hammie Rex. We were going to have to do this by ourselves.

"Hooray. My biggest customer came back," said Mr. Lomax, crossing his arms. "Did I say 'customer'? I meant 'vandal.' FYI, you forgot to start any fires the last time, in case you wanted to add arson to your rap sheet."

I sighed. "Not here for arson, sir," I said. "I just want to ask you a few questions. I'm trying to get to the bottom of this whole misunderstanding."

"What are you, some sort of boy detective?" said Mr. Lomax.

"I used to be," I said.

"Well, I've got a question for you, Sherlock Jr.,"

said Mr. Lomax. "How many weird little hamsters have you got hidden on you right now?"

"None," I said. "I promise." I unzipped my pack to show him that it was empty. I'd left Hamstersaurus Rex to keep watch on the sidewalk outside.

"Fine. Then I'm going to assume you brought the $624.25 you still owe me," said Mr. Lomax. He held out his hand.

"Not yet," I said. "I'm working on it."

"Well, you better work quick," said Mr. Lomax. "I don't want to have to bring the police into this."

"Can I just ask who put that display Snuzzle on the shelf?" I said.

"Pshaw. Display Snuzzle?" said Mr. Lomax. "That's how I knew your story was bunk the first time. There wasn't any 'display' Snuzzle."

"What?" I said. "I'm telling you there was!"

Mr. Lomax frowned as he checked the old computer by the register. "Nope," he said. "According to my inventory, my first shipment of Snuzzles came in today at three o'clock. I've got two hundred in the back waiting to go on sale tomorrow."

I was starting to feel insane. "There was a

Snuzzle here!" I said. "Can we look at the security footage again?"

So we did. As unclear as the surveillance video was, it definitely showed Hammie Rex smashing Gooboo the Snuzzle around the store. Mr. Lomax seemed confused now.

"That's impossible," said Mr. Lomax. "I didn't shelve that item. If I had I would have charged you for breaking it."

"Oh, I'm sure of that," I said. "Does your store have any other employees?"

"Nope," said Mr. Lomax. "I tried to hire a kid part-time once but he kept stealing the free mints."

"If they're free you can't—" I stopped myself. It wasn't worth it. "We need to figure out how that Snuzzle got on your shelf."

Mr. Lomax cocked his head to look sideways at me. "Maybe you brought it here," he said.

"I brought a toy that costs sixty-seven dollars into your store just so I could smash it?" I said.

"I don't know how juvenile delinquents like you get their kicks," said Mr. Lomax. "You lodged a Max Stomper: Arctic Detective action figure in the ceiling!" He pointed up. It was still there.

"Please," I said. "Can you just go back a little further in the tape?"

Mr. Lomax sighed and rewound the footage. We watched the camera pointed at the back shelf—where Gooboo was sitting, presumably plotting my destruction in his little computer chip brain. The time-stamped hours counted down as the occasional browsing customer sped by backward through the frame. Suddenly, the Snuzzle disappeared.

"Stop the tape!" I cried.

Mr. Lomax did.

"Now play," I said.

One second Gooboo's box wasn't sitting on the shelf; the next second it was. Huh?

"The time stamp is messed up," I said. "Looks like several minutes of footage are missing."

Mr. Lomax furrowed his brow. "Must be some kind of glitch," he said. "My inclination is to blame you."

"Mr. Lomax, whoever put that Snuzzle on the shelf is responsible for the damage to your store," I said. "Not me or Hamstersaurus Rex."

"How do I know that's true?" said Mr. Lomax, who seemed genuinely vexed now. "Maybe you had an accomplice, part of a bigger hamster-themed crime ring."

"Do you remember what was happening from

2:07 to 2:21 p.m.?" I said. "Did any customers come in?"

"Sure, I have an impeccably clear memory of that specific fourteen-minute span from two days ago," said Mr. Lomax. "Just as I'm sure you know exactly what you were doing from 11:36 to 11:43 a.m. last Sunday!"

"I was working on my screenplay, *The Swords of Hamstervalia*!" I said.

"Terrible title. Would not watch," said Mr. Lomax. "Regardless, maybe the manufacturer accidentally sent me a Snuzzle early, and I put it on the shelf and forgot about it." Even he didn't seem convinced by the explanation. "Look, this doesn't change a thing. You still disobeyed a store rule that is clearly posted on the door and you still owe me that money!"

But he was wrong. It did change something for me. I now knew that someone snuck into the toy store and somehow erased the security footage of themselves placing the killer Snuzzle on the shelf: oodles of creepy.

"Thanks for your help, Mr. Lomax," I said.

"You sure you don't want to buy some wax lips?" said Mr. Lomax as I rushed out the door. The good news was that I was getting closer to the truth. But there was still one more place I needed to go.

"C'mon, Hammie," I said. "Time to try a long shot." With a growl, the little guy somersaulted into my open backpack.

Not much later, Hamstersaurus Rex and I walked into the offices of Maple Bluffs Animal Control. I was taken aback by what I saw. The reception area was now packed with various tanks, cages, and terrariums of all shapes and sizes. Every one of them contained a strange hybrid animal that had escaped from SmilesCorp. The racket of their squawks, chirps, squeals, and grunts was overwhelming. Agent Gould sat there with a harried look on her face. The desk phone rang but she didn't pick up. Instead, she muttered something under her breath and sent the call straight to voice mail.

"Hi," I said as I approached. "I'm Sam Gibbs; we've met before. This is going to sound strange, but—"

"Let me guess," said Gould. "Your whole sequin collection got stolen in broad daylight by some sort of invisible, cackling beast?"

"Uh, no," I said. "That's way, *way* off."

"Oh, thank goodness," said Gould, breathing a sigh of relief. But her calm didn't last long. The phone immediately started ringing again. She rubbed her temples and sent this to voice mail, too.

Agent McKay stood by the coffeemaker, surrounded on all sides with cages full of scaly white mice. He looked even more frazzled than Gould. "So, are you here to report that weird hamster for being weird?"

Hamstersaurus Rex snorted and stuck out his tiny tongue.

"No," I said. "In fact, you guys should probably give Hamstersaurus Rex a medal or something for everything he's done for you."

"I seem to recall we wrote him a giant novelty check once?" said Gould.

"He couldn't cash it!" I said.

"Hey, here's an idea," said McKay, brightening. "Maybe as his reward, your hamster can take my job!" He started to unfasten his badge but Gould shot him a look that stopped him cold. McKay sighed.

"I don't get it," I said. "I thought you two loved working for Maple Bluffs Animal Control."

"Look around, kid," said Gould, indicating the wall-to-wall squawking mutants. "Does this appear to be a relaxing work environment to you?"

"Does seem a tad loud," I yelled over the racket.

"It's basically a mutant petting zoo in here!" cried McKay. "What are we supposed to do with them all?"

"I don't know," I said. "I'm just here to ask if you've heard any reports of a one-eyed robotic 'animal' on the loose: bat ears; antenna; extremely cute but in a slightly sickening way."

"Can't say as I have," said Gould. The phone rang again. She ignored it. "The only thing we're getting these days is complaints about the Chameleonkey."

"The Chameleonkey?" I said.

"We nabbed that dachshund with six legs,"

said McKay, pointing to a cage across the room that held a six-legged dog. "We cleared all the scaly mice out of Milos Schweyer's toolshed. We

somehow managed to build a case file on the chicken that looked exactly like a turtle and apprehend it." He indicated a terrarium with a turtle in it. The turtle clucked. "All the weirdo critters that escaped from the SmilesCorp Genetic Research and Development Lab have now been caught. Except one."

"Half chameleon, half spider monkey, all mischief," said Gould. "Thanks to its natural camouflage, the Chameleonkey can effectively render itself invisible at will. And the fuzzy little fugitive has a penchant for larceny. Loves stealing the shiniest of shinies: hologram stickers, chocolate coins, bedazzled phone cases, you name it, buster."

"The Chameleonkey keeps hitting the Maple Bluffs flea market to steal handfuls of worthless yet sparkly junk," said McKay. "It's making the two of us look like fools."

In my experience, making Agents Gould and McKay look like fools wasn't exactly the toughest thing in the world to accomplish. But I didn't say so.

"Don't get us wrong, kid," said Gould. "We're the best there is at what we do."

"We've been on the cover of *Animal Control Monthly* twice," said McKay, puffing. "And Gould made the style section for her fashion-forward sock choices."

"Most animal control agents would never consider wearing paisley," said Gould. "But the Chameleonkey, well . . . this might just be the case that breaks us."

"Verminator Two, this is Verminator One," said McKay, shaking his head. "Come in for a hug." With a heavy mutual sigh, Gould and McKay gave each other a sad hug. The phone started ringing again.

Suddenly, an idea struck me. "Hey, Hamstersaurus Rex and I have been pretty good at tracking down these rogue SmilesCorp mutants in the past," I said. "In fact, it's kind of our specialty. Is there any sort of reward for catching the Chameleonkey?"

"You'd earn our undying respect," said McKay, and he started to salute.

"Awesome," I said, "but I need cash."

"Well, we are authorized to offer a monetary reward for the capture of any rogue animal we deem to be 'highly elusive,'" said Gould. "Just like the bounty we once mistakenly put on your little hamster buddy there. Boy, wasn't that a hoot?" Gould chuckled.

"Better days," said McKay. "Better days."

Hamstersaurus Rex snarled.

"So how much are we talking?" I said.

"Three hundred dollars," said Gould. "Payable in cash this time if it's more convenient."

"All right," I said. "We'll do it."

Three hundred dollars would put me halfway to being square with Mr. Lomax. After you'd faced down a squirrel the size of a grizzly bear and a mole with telekinetic mind powers, how tough could capturing an invisible monkey be?

It wasn't until I walked out the door, beaming, that I remembered I hadn't learned anything about the evil Snuzzle. It was getting dark as Hamstersaurus Rex and I started to walk home. I couldn't help but glance over my shoulder every few blocks. Somewhere out there was a robotic killing machine that couldn't say its *r*'s.

CHAPTER 5

THE NEXT MORNING, I went straight to the school library to put Hamstersaurus Rex into the PETCATRAZ Pro™ with the rest of his hamster family. Stompy, Chompy, and Hatshepsut were practically vibrating with excitement and Hammie was thrilled to see them, too. Even Cartimandua gave a little mid-nap smile.

"Good morning, little dudes, glad to see we all made it safely through the night without any troub—"

"WADICAL, BWO!"

I froze as those creepy, warbling words drifted into the library from the hallway. There was no mistaking the voice: it was definitely a Snuzzle. The thing *had* tracked me here after all!

"Mrs. Baxley!" I cried. "We're under attack! Help me bar the door." I started to roll a heavy book cart to block the library's main entrance.

"Sam, I am in the process of reshelving those titles," said Mrs. Baxley, stomping on the book cart's brake lever. "Go build a barricade somewhere else."

"Okay, but just promise me you'll protect the

baby hamsters while I investigate!" I said. "You're a Hamster Monitor now!"

"Am not," said Mrs. Baxley, as she put a hardback copy of *Day of the Cackle* back onto the shelf.

There was no time to argue. I snatched Hammie Rex and we cautiously crept out into the hallway.

I saw a Snuzzle. Then another. And another. It looked like every kid at Horace Hotwater was cuddling one of the things as they blinked their oversized eyes and warbled gibberish like "I WUV

YOU" and "MY NOSE IS FUZZY-WUZZY."

Hamstersaurus Rex gave a low growl. He was right. It was time to act.

"Keeeeeagh!" I yelled as I slapped the Snuzzle out of Omar Powell's hands, sending it clattering down the hallway. "Save yourself, Omar!"

"Sam, what are you doing?" cried Omar, horrified.

"That thing is going to turn on you any second," I cried. "But I'm here to help!"

By this time, Omar's Snuzzle had righted itself and started to toddle back toward him.

"Sic 'im, boy!" I yelled. With a snarl, Hammie Rex tackled Omar's Snuzzle and pinned it to the ground.

"It's not going to turn on me," said Omar as he tried to wrestle the Snuzzle away from Hammie. "It just told me it 'wuvs' me!"

"What's all the commotion?" said Caroline Moody. She approached cradling another cooing Snuzzle in her arms.

"Caroline, smash that Snuzzle before it bites your face off!" I said. "If you can't do it, I will!

Somebody get me a hammer!" Nobody did.

"MY TOES AWE VEWY TICKWISH," said Caroline's Snuzzle.

"Have you lost your mind?" said Caroline. "My Snuzzle is named Oobie and I gave it a French braid and now it's my best friend!"

"I thought I was your best friend," said Tina Gomez, frowning.

"We can talk later," said Caroline.

"Give me that thing!" I cried. "I'm going to destroy it! You'll thank me!" I lunged for her Snuzzle when something caught me by the collar in midair.

"What exactly seems to be the trouble here, Mr. Gibbs?" said Principal Truitt.

Before I could answer, Jimmy Choi stepped forward. "Ahem. I saw the whole thing, ma'am," said Jimmy (of course holding his own Snuzzle). "Sam is trying to smash our toys. Possibly because he hates fun."

"Is this true?" said Principal Truitt. "Do you hate fun?"

"No," I said. "These Snuzzles are dangerous!"

"I WIKE FWESHWY BAKED CHOCOWATE CHIP COOKIES," said Omar's Snuzzle, from underneath Hammie Rex.

"Annoying, perhaps," said Principal Truitt, "but they don't seem dangerous."

"They're trying to lure us into a false sense of security," I said. "Waiting for the right moment to strike!"

"CAN I GIVE YOU A WITTWE SMOOCH?" said Jimmy's Snuzzle.

"CEWTAINWY!" said Caroline's Snuzzle, demonstrating the toys' much-hyped ability to wirelessly interface and talk to one another.

"Riiiight," said Principal Truitt. "And why is Hamstersaurus Rex out of his designated Hamster Habitat?"

"He was, er, helping me battle this evil menace and, you know, save the school," I said. "Just like how he saved the school last—"

"We all remember, Mr. Gibbs," said Principal Truitt, with a touch of irritation creeping into her voice. "But Horace Hotwater has enjoyed months of uninterrupted calm and safety now. Perhaps it's time to dispense with the heroics and focus on schoolwork?"

Principal Truitt nudged Hammie Rex aside and picked up Omar's Snuzzle. She eyed it.

"SKATEBOAWDING IS COOL," said the Snuzzle.

"I happen to disagree," said Principal Truitt. "But this is clearly a harmless child's toy, Mr. Gibbs."

"If I may, ma'am," said Caroline. "It's actually the ultimate twenty-first-century smartpet experience."

"Mmm," said Principal Truitt. "Well, I don't want any more disturbances like this in the future, so no more Snuzzles in the halls or classrooms. Keep them stowed in your lockers during school hours or better yet, leave them at home."

This elicited a communal groan from all the Snuzzle owners.

"And I'm going to need you to put Hamstersaurus Rex back in his enclosure, Mr. Gibbs," said Principal Truitt. "Now." She turned and strode off down the hallway.

"Thanks a lot, Sam," said Omar as his Snuzzle toddled back toward him.

"I'm not the bad guy here!" I said. But I had to admit: none of the Snuzzles seemed to be displaying any of the homicidal tendencies of the one that attacked me. They were mostly nuzzling and cooing. I gathered Hammie up and started back toward the library.

"Well, okay, maybe I was wrong," I said to the little guy. "Maybe it was just some sort of freak one-in-a-zillion malfunction that caused the Snuzzle at Tenth Street Toys to attack me. And maybe it was just the wind I heard in the bushes the other afternoon?"

Hamstersaurus Rex grunted. From the look in his eye, the little guy didn't seem convinced. Still, if Snuzzles weren't an immediate threat, that was a good thing, wasn't it? It meant I could focus on the nigh-impossible task of coming up with six hundred dollars that I (unjustly) owed a grumpy toy store owner. Ugh.

At lunch I put my tray down beside Dylan and Martha. "Guys, I need your help!"

"Well, that's creamed corn. The green stuff is supposed to be spinach. And I think the thing in the middle is baked ziti," said Dylan, pointing out the various food items on my tray.

"No, not identifying cafeteria food," I said. "I need your help catching a mutant spider monkey! Just like old times!"

Martha and Dylan looked at me like I was crazy. Still, I've noticed that every time you have to explain to your friends why it's important to track down a freaky mutant creature that's causing trouble it gets a little easier. I told them everything I knew about the so-called Chameleonkey: its camouflage, its preoccupation with shiny objects, and how the reward money was my only path to paying back Mr. Lomax for the damage to the store. ". . . So in conclusion," I said, "I think we ought to set a trap at the Maple Bluffs Flea Market on Saturday."

"This Saturday?" said Martha. "I can't."

"Huh?" I said. "Why not?"

"Well, since my grades have been utterly ruined," she said, "my only hope to get into the

Sorbonne's veterinary sciences program is to double down on my e-curricks."

"E-curricks?" said Dylan.

"Sorry. I mean my extracurriculars," said Martha. "I was attempting to use slang, as we young people are known to do."

"But, Martha, you already have so many e-curricks!" I said. "What about competitive origami? What about glassblowing decathlon? What about interpretive jousting?"

"It's not enough!" said Martha. "I need to lead a winning Model Interplanetary Council delegation or I'll never fulfill my dream career trajectory of horse vet, volcanologist, president, CEO, president."

"You said president twice," I said.

"I assume we will have had a female president by the time I'm thirty-five," said Martha. "So the only meaningful barrier left for me to break will be first female *nonconsecutive* president. You know, two different terms, like Grover Cleveland. Anyway, my Horace Hotwater Model Interplanetary Council team is practicing all day that day."

"Well, good luck with whatever that is," I said. "How about you, Dylan? Can I count on your help or does seven years of friendship mean nothing these days?"

"You're in luck," said Dylan. "It means I can spare a little time this Saturday to help you capture the Chameleonkey. I'm going to be near the Maple Bluffs Flea Market that morning anyway."

By remaining extremely vague, I was also able to convince Serena to help. All I had to do was pitch the idea to her in the form of a misleading internet headline: "You'll Never Believe What's Been Happening at the Flea Market, But Once You Do Your Heart Will Melt!" I told her the potential for viral video content was high. I invited Beefer to come along, too. An extra set of hands might be useful (even if they were unconnected to any sort of brain). Of course Hamstersaurus Rex—my steadfast partner in every adventure—would be there as always.

On Saturday morning, I left Cartimandua and the pups in the hamster habitat in my garage and rode my bike to the Maple Bluffs Flea Market with

Hamstersaurus Rex. The market happened every week in the big parking lot next to Windchime's Organic Foods. As far as the eye could see, shoppers browsed tables piled high with comic books, old toys, vinyl records, secondhand clothes, and pretty much anything else under the sun. As I waited for the others, I tried to resist the urge to buy a windup moose for fifty cents, even though it was pretty cool. While I was weighing the pros and cons, Hammie Rex accidentally knocked over a whole row of Hawaiian-themed nutcrackers. I was picking them up as Serena arrived.

"Heya, Sam," said Serena. "What's happening, Spikehead, otherwise known as Hammie Rex?" She filmed the market with her smartphone as she arrived. "Wow, this place is great! So kitschy!"

"Yep," I said. "You can find whatever you want here. As long as you didn't mind it smelling like it's been in somebody's garage for the last thirty years."

"I beg your pardon," said the nutcracker vendor, who could apparently hear me.

"Sorry," I said.

"Ooh, cool windup moose!" said Serena as she zoomed in with her camera. "How much?"

"Ninja reveal GO!" yelled Beefer, startling us both as he leaped out from behind a stack of old board games. He struck a ninja pose and held it for a long moment while Serena and I stared at him.

". . . Cool?" I said.

"You're darn tootin' it is," said Beefer. "Okay, let's get this show on the road. Who am I supposed to ninja chop and/or ninja bite?"

"Nobody," I said. "Our goal is the nonviolent capture of the elusive Chameleonkey."

"Fine," said Beefer. "But you owe me big-time for this, Sam!"

"You haven't even *done* anything yet," I said.

"I took time out of my busy schedule to come help you," said Beefer. "Time is a ninja's most valuable resource." He bowed.

"Oh yeah?" said Serena, turning the camera on Beefer now. "What else you got on the docket today, chief?"

"Lots of . . . friend events," said Beefer. "I have friends!"

"Sure you do," said Serena, still filming.

"Hey, look. It's Dylan," I said.

Indeed, she was making her way through the crowd, wearing a brand-new visor. Right behind her was Drew McCoy, wearing the same brand-new visor.

"Drew?" I said under my breath. "Seriously?"

"Hey, guys," said Dylan. "Serena, this is Drew."

"Yo," said Serena. "Cool visors."

"Yeah," said Dylan. "They were having a big sale at Visor Vizier. Figured we should pick up a matching pair before disc golf camp."

"It's not a fedora but I could get used to it," said Drew, touching the bare top of his head. "The design really lets the scalp breathe, you know?"

Dylan (and nobody else) burst out laughing.

"Have we met?" said Beefer.

"Yes, at your bar mitzvah the other day," said Drew. "And also we went to school together for several years before that."

"Not ringing a bell," said Beefer. "I'm Beefer."

"'Sup," said Drew. "I'm Drew."

"Okay, guys, we're all here," I said. "So

apparently the Chameleonkey can't resist anything sparkly. That means we need to stake out the shiniest table here."

"Ah, then you kids should go find Madame Karla," said the nutcracker vendor, who was apparently still eavesdropping on our conversation.

He was right, though. We soon found a woman draped in brightly colored scarves manning a table piled high with gaudy costume jewelry.

"Bingo," I said.

"Wow," said Serena, zooming in on a brooch that looked like a hamburger, "this stuff is hilarious."

"And what exactly do you mean by that, young lady?" said Madame Karla.

"What she means is: Have you had any trouble with the Chameleonkey recently, ma'am?" I said.

"Indeed I have," said Madame Karla with a snort. "Every week! Last time the abominable beast made off with several sapphire-style amulets and an invaluable three-dollar mood ring!"

"Well, we're here to help," I said.

"I'm a ninja of untold power," said Beefer.

Madame Karla cocked her head.

"And more importantly, I'm a respected digital journalist who had a very successful blog post," said Serena, now aiming her smartphone at Madame Karla. "As you are the unfortunate victim of these horrible attacks, I'd like to learn

more about your sad, sad life. You know, human interest stuff."

"Eh?" said Madame Karla. "Okay."

"So tell me what it's like to be a struggling fake jewelry vendor, just trying to make ends meet?" said Serena.

"I'm not struggling," said Madame Karla. "I'm a successful optometrist who does this for fun on the weekends."

"Hmm," said Serena, turning off the camera.

"Okay," I said, "so maybe we should take up our positions around the perimeter of the—"

"Two matching charm bracelets, please!" said Dylan, plunking down five bucks on Madame Karla's table.

Madame Karla handed her two cheap-looking bracelets. Dylan smiled and gave one to Drew.

"Oh wow, Dylan!" said Drew. "Pretty soon all our clothes will match!"

"Now we have to pick out our charms," said Dylan. "Madame Karla, do you have any shaped like disc golf discs?"

"Or fedoras?" asked Drew.

"Hey, can we try to stay focused for one minute?" I said.

"Sam, that reminds me: this flea market would be a great place for you to get me a gift," said Beefer, looking around. "Since you very inconsiderately didn't get me anything for my bar mitzvah. I did see a guy selling some sweet battle-axes back there—"

"Beefer, I don't have any cash to spare for medieval weaponry!" I said. "I'm six hundred bucks in the hole. That's the whole point of trying to catch the Chameleonkey, so I can claim the reward money and pay back—"

"There's reward money?" said Beefer.

"Well . . . yeah," I said.

"Then I demand half!" said Beefer.

"Children," said Madame Karla.

"Hang on. If Beefer gets half, then I want half," said Dylan. "Well, a fifth. Because there are five of us."

I hadn't considered my friends would want a cut of the Chameleonkey's bounty. "Ugh," I said. "Look, we can discuss maybe, *possibly* dividing up the money later."

"The fair thing to do would be to recognize your friends' contributions," said Dylan, her eyes narrowing.

"But the whole point of claiming this reward is so I'll have enough cash for the toy store!" I said.

"Oh, so you need all the money so you can go buy toys with it?" said Beefer, shaking his head. "That's just greedy, Sam."

"I'm not buying toys with it!" I said.

"Drew and I are going to use our shares to buy matching scarves," said Dylan.

"You read my mind!" said Drew.

"Look," I said. "I didn't even invite Drew, so obviously he's not getting a share!"

"You didn't invite me?" said Drew.

Dylan glared at me now.

"Children!" said Madame Karla.

"Sam, we are risking our necks to catch this invisible monkey and we should be fairly compensated," said Beefer. "I'm about to strike. Who's with me?"

"Nobody's risking their necks!" I said. "The

invisible monkey isn't dangerous."

"Hang on," said Serena. "The monkey's invisible."

I winced. "Yes," I said. "It's SmilesCorp Specimen #85882. *Chameleonidae cebus*."

Serena glared at me. "Sam, how am I supposed to get viral-ready HD video content of something that is invisible?" she said.

"Hmm. Maybe turn this whole thing into a podcast?" offered Drew.

"CHILDREN!" cried Madame Karla.

"What?" we all said in unison.

"The Chameleonkey!" cried Madame Karla. "It has arrived!"

CHAPTER 6

ON THE FAR corner of Madame Karla's table, the gaudy fake jewelry seemed to be rifling through itself. The hamburger brooch slowly floated off the table. The effect was eerie, to say the least.

"It's . . . it's . . . it's the ghost of Horace Hotwater!" hissed Beefer.

"Dude, don't even start with that!" I said. "It's the Chameleonkey!"

"So, uh, what do we do?" said Dylan.

"Get it!" I cried.

Hamstersaurus Rex roared and flew at the Chameleonkey, but at the last second the invisible monkey let out a cackle and leaped . . . somewhere.

"Follow that Chameleonkey!" I cried. "Don't let it out of your sight!"

"It was never *in* our sight!" said Dylan, scanning the flea market.

I heard another telltale cackle. I turned to see the brooch bobbing above a rack of vintage Astro-Robo toys across the aisle.

"There!" I started to run. "Split up and keep an eye on the brooch!"

Dylan and Drew broke left. Beefer and Serena went right. Hamstersaurus Rex and I ran straight ahead, dodging through the crowded aisles and trying to cut off the Chameleonkey's escape route. The brooch bounced from a rack of novelty T-shirts, to a bin of antique sporting goods, on to a shelf holding dozens of porcelain Baby President

figurines. The Chameleonkey cackled and leaped again, tipping the shelf over and shattering Washington through Polk.

I watched the levitating brooch land on top of a tent housing a bowling memorabilia vendor. Hamstersaurus Rex and I ran underneath.

"Hey, are you here to buy bowling cards?" said a large, goateed man in a bowling shirt who was suddenly blocking our path.

"Er, just browsing, sir," I said, keeping an eye on the tent above me. The Chameleonkey had stopped.

"Well, check out this Mikey Mayfield rookie card!" said the goateed man, holding up a card that depicted another large, goateed man in a bowling shirt. "Only nine bucks!"

Above us, the Chameleonkey broke left.

"Sorry, got to go!" I said.

"I haven't sold anything in three months!" the man wailed.

"Dylan, I think it's headed your way," I cried as Hamstersaurus Rex and I backtracked. Up ahead, I saw Dylan and Drew casually browsing a selection of knitted scarves.

"Ooh, I think this scarf is perfect," said Drew, holding one up. "Or should I say . . . *scarf-ect*."

Dylan laughed heartily at what may have charitably been described as Drew's joke.

"What are two you even doing?" I yelled.

Dylan and Drew looked startled. "Whoa, sorry, Sam, we were just picking out scarves," said Dylan. "Drew's way into stripes. But I think polka dots are pretty underrated."

"We go back and forth," said Drew. "It's cute."

"I'll take your word for it!" I cried as Hammie and I jogged past. "In the meantime, you let the Chameleonkey get away!"

Up ahead I came to a four-way intersection of aisles. I had no idea where the Chameleonkey had gone. A second later, Beefer and Serena came running from the right.

"Did you lose the little invisible weirdo?" asked Serena.

"Yep," I said.

"Ugh, Sam, you just cost me my reward money," said Beefer. "So inconsiderate."

Just then we heard a bloodcurdling scream of

terror. Serena, Hammie, Beefer, and I looked at each other. Then we ran in the general direction of the scream.

A few aisles over we found a man who looked genuinely shell-shocked, standing by a rack of sunglasses.

"Sir, what happened?" I said.

"I was trying on a pair of 1997 New Year's Eve novelty glasses," said the man, "when all of a sudden they just flew off my head!"

"No need to worry," I said, "there's an invisible monkey on the loose."

A look of absolute terror spread across the man's face. ". . . I just thought somebody was playing a prank on me," he said, looking around. "An invisible monkey? That's much, *much* more alarming!"

"Sorry," I said.

"Up there!" cried Serena, pointing with her smartphone.

About fifty feet away, Madame Karla's brooch and pair of sparkly sunglasses in the shape of the year 1997—the eyes were the holes of the two

9s—floated above one of the parking lot's twenty-foot-tall light poles.

"How do we even get up there?" I said.

"Anybody know how to levitate?" said Serena.

"The one day I forget my grappling hook . . . ," said Beefer.

"Hammie, can you climb it?" I said.

Hammie Rex looked a little uncertain, but then he barked in the affirmative. At least he was ready to try.

"No need," said Beefer, stepping forward. "Even without a rope, climbing sheer surfaces is basic Ninja 101 stuff."

"Are you sure we shouldn't send the little guy?" I said. "We're only going to get one shot at—"

"No time for discussion! I'm about to *earn* that reward money!" cried Beefer, and he backed up and pulled his ninja mask

over his head. "You're welcome." Then he took a running go at the light pole.

"Beefer, wait!" I cried, but it was too late.

"Spinning ninja jump-climb maneuver GO!" yelled Beefer as he launched himself at the light pole. Instead of climbing up it, though, he kind of awkwardly swung around it once, then twice, building momentum with each revolution.

"Oh no," I said.

"Oh yes," said Serena. Her phone camera was trained squarely on Beefer as he spun around it a third and final time before letting go and flying wildly through the air. He sailed about fifteen feet before smashing directly into a heavy bin full of Beanie Buddy stuffed animals. The Beanie Buddies went flying and a nearby rack—holding used kitchen appliances—tipped over. The whole thing fell right on top of Beefer with a horrendous crash.

The noise startled the Chameleonkey. With one final cackle, the creature sprang off the light pole, onto a tent, then onto another tent, where it vaulted into the woods beside the parking lot and disappeared for good.

A second later, Hammie, Serena, and I caught up to Beefer. He was nearly buried under Beanie Buddies and old food processors.

". . . Did I win Science Night?" asked Beefer, who seemed dazed.

"Nope," I said. "And the Chameleonkey got away." Hammie Rex gave a frustrated growl and kicked a pebble hard enough to send it sailing over the flea market.

"Well, luckily one thing did get caught," said Serena. "That whole spinning ninja thing, on video." She replayed the footage on her phone and her eyes lit up. "This has got to be the most spectacular thing I've ever seen."

"Spectacularly . . . good?" said Beefer.

"Oh no," said Serena. "The opposite of that." She showed him the clip (which she had already color-balanced and edited for clarity). On-screen,

Beefer pulled on his mask and ran, then twirled around like a rag doll and flung himself at high speed into a big pile of stuffed animals. "Folks, I think I have my next blog post," said Serena, eyeing her phone like it was a bar of pure gold.

"What? That's not journalism," said Beefer. "Don't post that!"

"Too late," said Serena. "Just did. They make it so easy."

"But I didn't sign a release!" wailed Beefer.

Dylan and Drew strolled up, of course now sporting matching plaid scarves.

"Did you guys catch the Chameleonkey?" said Dylan.

"Of course we didn't," I said. "But I'm glad to see you got your scarves!"

"Thanks," said Drew, fluffing his. "I realized plaid is just, like, double the stripes."

"I was being sarcastic!" I said.

"Sam, I'm not sure why it's so important for the rest of us to bankroll your property damage anyway," said Dylan, stepping between Drew and me. "Seems like this toy store thing is *your* problem. We were just being nice by trying to help."

"Oh, were you?" I said. "So when exactly were you going to try to help?"

Dylan glared.

"Oh man, it's already up to six thousand hits," said Serena.

"Serena, take it down!" said Beefer. "I'm worried someone will see that video and mistakenly think I'm foolish."

"Ten thousand hits!" said Serena, pumping her fist.

"Enough with the web traffic updates!" I snapped, startling everyone. "It's not *news* that Beefer did something stupid and messed everything up!"

"Hey!" said Beefer.

"Yikes," said Serena.

I realized that they were all staring at me now, even Hamstersaurus Rex.

I took a deep breath. "You know what," I said, "it seems like you all have a lot going on right now. So I think from here on out, maybe Hammie and I will just try to handle this Chameleonkey thing ourselves."

Before anyone could say anything, I turned and left.

"Why so glum, Bunnybutt?" said my mom as I walked in the front door.

"No reason," I said. "Just realized I don't have any *real* friends."

"Oh, is that all?" said my mom. "Well, we can have pizza tonight if you want. Pizza's better than friends."

"Thanks," I said.

My mom sniffled a little. "I'm guessing Hamstersaurus Rex is in the garage?" She was highly allergic to anything with fur, even mutant dinohamsters. Thankfully I'd constructed a homemade hypoallergenic habitat (patent pending) that mitigated the worst of it.

"Yep," I said. "Cartimandua and the kids are here, too."

"I'll be sure to order an extra pie, then," she said.

I spent the afternoon tinkering with *The Swords*

of Hamstervalia. By dinnertime, I had changed the title to *A Hamster Alone*. It was now the melancholy tale of the last hamster on earth, after an apocalypse where bees sting everyone to death. I still hadn't written any of it, though. Mom and I had pizza from Vito's and watched a movie about aliens trying to run a shoe store but none of it made me feel much better. After dinner I took the spare pie out to Hammie Rex and his family.

Stompy, Chompy, and Hatshepsut were no slouches when it came to scarfing pizza. The pups could eat. Cartimandua gingerly nibbled at a basil leaf and Hammie Rex beamed with pride as he watched his kids gobble slice after slice of pepperoni and mushroom. It struck me that even Hamstersaurus Rex had his own priorities these days.

I went to bed feeling unsettled. I still had no idea how I was going to get the rest of the money that I owed to Mr. Lomax, which was so unfair anyway. I considered asking my mom for it, but she'd taken a big pay cut with her new job. That was also unfair. Everything: unfair . . .

I awoke with a start at 3:07 a.m. Or was it 8:19? The digits on my clock radio shifted strangely. Outside, I heard a noise. I crept out of bed and made my way to the window. In the glow of the streetlights I could see a small, furry creature crossing my front yard.

I opened the window. "Hammie . . . is that you?" I whispered.

The creature froze. Then slowly it looked up at me with one glowing red eye.

"DESTWOY," it said.

CHAPTER 7

I MADE IT DOWNSTAIRS and out into the yard in time to see the Snuzzle wedge its little paws underneath the garage door. With a crunching noise, it wrenched the door six inches upward.

"Don't do that, you're going to break it, mister!" I yelled (a line that sounded way more heroic and intimidating in my head).

The Snuzzle turned to face me, its dangling eye sparking occasionally. "DESTW—"

WHANG! I hit the Snuzzle right in the forehead with a toy car launched from my oversized slingshot (thanks, birthday money!). The Snuzzle staggered backward, stunned. Its good eye blinked.

"There's more where that came from, pal!" I said. "These pajama pockets are full of my hardest, pointiest toys!"

The Snuzzle squinted its glowing red eye. But instead of charging, it turned and ripped a three-foot section of the gutter off the side of the house.

"Whoa, hey! Come on!" I said. "My allowance depends on cleaning those!" I launched another toy car, but this time the Snuzzle swung the gutter like a baseball bat and knocked it right back at me. I had to dive to avoid taking a two-inch hot rod to the face!

"DISENGAGE SECONDAWY TAWGET," said the Snuzzle, dropping the gutter bat. "OBJECTIVE: DESTWOY PWIMAWY TAWGET."

It turned back toward the garage door. With another wrenching yank, the Snuzzle raised it far enough to walk through and—

WHAM! From out of the dark garage, Hamstersaurus Rex smashed into the Snuzzle, knocking the evil toy across the yard. Stompy, Chompy, and Hatshepsut came charging out right behind their dad, snarling and growling and generally trying to look tough. They might each only be one-quarter dinosaur, but they had inherited all of Hamstersaurus Rex's fighting spirit.

With mechanical precision, the Snuzzle flipped onto its feet and then sprang high into the air. I lost sight of it in the glow of the streetlight. THUD! At the last second, Hamstersaurus Rex rolled out of the way as the Snuzzle smashed the dirt with its balled fist. Hammie opened his jaws for a monster chomp, but the Snuzzle twirled and kicked him in the face, sending him reeling. The Snuzzle picked up the section of gutter to bash Hammie.

From behind it came a tiny roar, a few octaves higher than Hammie's. Chompy had clamped his jaws right onto the Snuzzle's fuzzy backside. The Snuzzle seemed confused for a moment. Then, with blinding speed, the Snuzzle swatted Chompy away. The hamster pup squeaked as he rolled across the yard.

Hamstersaurus Rex let out a roar loud enough to wake up the whole neighborhood, possibly the state. Now his eyes almost seemed to glow with pure rage as he flew at the Snuzzle and—at the last instant—spun his dino-tail like a whip. KAPOW! The blow smashed the Snuzzle against the trunk of our oak tree, with a metallic crunch. The gutter bat went spinning away.

"WAWNING!" said the Snuzzle. "SEVEWE DAMAGE TO ALL SYST—"

KERSMASH! Hamstersaurus Rex kicked the Snuzzle's chest with both feet. The impact popped the Snuzzle's right arm off and sent it flying.

"EWWOR! EWWOR! . . . IMMINENT SYSTEM FAIWUWE DUE TO CATASWTOPHIC DAMAGE . . . ," said the Snuzzle.

Hamstersaurus Rex snarled and smashed the Snuzzle again, and again. I'd never seen the little guy go berserk like this, not on Squirrel Kong, not on the Mind Mole, heck, not even on a bag of Funchos Marinara and Cream Cheese Flavor-Wedges! The threat to his pups had pushed Hammie over the edge. He roared and head-butted the Snuzzle, over and over. He didn't stop until the toy was pulverized beyond all recognition.

"DESTWOOOOoooooooooo . . . can I give you a wittwe smooocchhhgggh . . . ?" said the Snuzzle, its voice slowly fading. The sinister red light of its eye dimmed and then, at last, went dark.

Without wasting an instant, Hamstersaurus Rex darted across the yard to Chompy's side. I jogged after him. The little pup looked banged up but—as far as I could tell—there was no real harm done. He seemed nearly as mad as his dad about the whole thing.

"You survived your first robot punch," I said. "Not bad."

Hamstersaurus Rex cuddled Chompy close and licked his fur. Stompy, Hatshepsut, and even

Cartimandua joined the group hug. I noticed now that Hammie Rex was shaking as the adrenaline of the fight wore off. The little guy was terrified for the safety of his kids. I knew what I had to do.

"Hammie, Cartimandua, don't worry," I said. "From now on I promise I'll keep your pups out of harm's way, no matter what."

I didn't have occasion to show it much these days, but I pulled out my official Hamster Monitor ID card.

"I swear it on this sacred lanyard," I said.

Hamstersaurus Rex looked up at me with tears welling in his eyes. Chompy yipped.

"Sorry, little dudes," I said. "I know you want to have adventures and stuff, but right now you're just too young."

Stompy kicked some dirt. Hatshepsut blew a miniature hamster raspberry.

"Sam, what on earth is going on out here?" said my mom, who was standing on the front step.

"An adorable-yet-evil robot was attacking the garage but Hammie Rex kicked its stupid butt," I said.

"Oh good. But you need to come inside, son, it's the middle of the—ACHOOOOOOO!" My mom let out one of her earth-shattering sneezes. Lights started to go on around the neighborhood. If anyone had managed to sleep through the fight of the century, they were awake now.

"Don't worry, Mom," I said. "I'll go back to bed soon."

I quickly ushered the hamster family back into the garage. They were shaken but glad to be snuggled together in their habitat. I locked the garage door behind me, and put my bike lock on it, too, for good measure. Then I breathed a sigh of relief: the evil Snuzzle menace was finally vanquished.

On my way back into the house, I gathered up what was left of the ultimate twenty-first-century smartpet experience: a lumpy mass of fake fur, shattered plastic, and dangling wires. The Snuzzle may have been defeated, but now I knew one thing for sure: it had a mission. Someone had intentionally programmed it to attack. And it wasn't after me. It's pwimawy tawge—er, its *primary target* was Hamstersaurus Rex!

The next morning, I called the only person I could think of who might be able to help me get to the bottom of the mystery: Martha Cherie. Her mother answered the phone and politely informed me that Martha was not home. She had several "e-currick" practices that day—Math Chorale, Linear A Club, and of course, Model Interplanetary Council—and would be in and out all day long, no way of predicting when. Martha organized her own schedule. I called back several times, trying to catch her. Not sure what Ms. Cherie thought the fourth time I gave her the message: "I need Martha to examine the murderous toy that attacked Hamstersaurus Rex!" By the fifth dial, my calls to the Cherie residence were going straight to their answering machine. I sighed.

I considered calling my other friends—Dylan was, after all, a Hamster Monitor, too—but I was still annoyed with them. I figured they'd just blow me off anyway. Jerks. Instead, I tossed the broken remnants of the Snuzzle into my backpack for later study and decided to focus on a much less important task: earning a bunch of stupid money.

The damage the Snuzzle–hamster battle had done to our front lawn gave me a great idea of how to make some cash, though. Most everyone in town had a yard. Nobody liked mowing it. Surely they'd pay someone like me to do that unwanted task for them. And at fifteen dollars a lawn, I'd only need to mow . . . well, honestly, it was better not to think about how many lawns I'd have to mow. I didn't want to get depressed. But after I mowed that unspecified (probably quite large) number of lawns, I'd be able to pay back Mr. Lomax. Maybe.

So Hamstersaurus Rex and I went door-to-door, asking if any of the neighbors needed grass clipped. Entrepreneurial lesson: when attempting to drum up new business, perhaps it's not the smartest idea to have a mutant dinosaur-hamster hybrid perched on your shoulder, especially one that has recently woken up the whole neighborhood in the middle of the night. I lost count of the nervous refusals and irritated door slams. Eventually I found myself several blocks from home, standing at the weathered door of a house I knew all too well. It had the most overgrown yard in all of Maple Bluffs.

"If this guy doesn't need our professional landscaping services, nobody will," I said. Hammie Rex nodded. I knocked.

The door swung open and there stood Old Man Ohlman, still sporting his trademark tinfoil hat.

"Good afternoon, Old M—er, Mr. Ohlman," I said. "You remember me!"

"Of course," said Old Man Ohlman. "You're Lt. Col. Conrad 'Tiny' Burton, the world's first child astronaut!" He gave a crisp salute.

"No, that's not me," I said.

"Are you Bryan Stokes, the boy who's never tasted candy?" said Old Man Ohlman, shaking his head. "So sad. So very sad. I have some licorice. It's pretty old but I reckon I could wipe the dust off it."

"No, I'm—"

"Augustine D. Katz Jr., heir to the Katz dog grooming fortune?" said Old Man Ohlman, doffing his hat.

"I'm Sam Gibbs!" I said quickly, before he could

take another guess.

"Sam Gibbs," said Old Man Ohlman. ". . . From the phone company?"

"No!" I said. "Okay, so remember that evil mole that attempted to mind-control you—"

"You're going to have to be more specific," said Old Man Ohlman.

"Doesn't matter," I said. "Anyway, I'm Sam Gibbs and this is my friend—"

"Oh, I'd recognize Hamstersaurus Rex anywhere!" said Old Man Ohlman. He extended his hand. Hammie looked at me quizzically, then stuck out a tiny dino-paw to shake it.

"How're the kids, HR?" said Old Man Ohlman. "Any big summer plans?"

Hamstersaurus Rex gave a confused grunt. Old Man Ohlman laughed.

"Never one to mince words, were you, Hammie? That's what I like about you," said Old Man Ohlman. "You and Cartimandua should come over for dinner sometime! We can all split one giant pancake."

"Anyway, sir," I said, "we were wondering if

you might need some yard work done."

Old Man Ohlman squinted at me and dropped his smile. "Son, are you saying the condition of my lawn is anything less than immaculate?"

I looked out over the grass, which was at least a foot high. The only spots where it wasn't a problem was where it had been killed by the clumps of thorny weeds that poked out of the ground. His mailbox was hidden under a mound of kudzu and I was pretty sure most of his flower bed was milkweed.

"The poison ivy in the side yard looks a little tall," I said mildly.

"Wait, this one is my yard?" said Old Man Ohlman, aghast. "I thought mine was that one over there." He pointed to a well-manicured lawn two houses down. "Well, okay, son, you're hired." He gasped. "You know, if this one is my front yard, I'm guessing my backyard is probably gonna be a doozy."

True enough, somehow Old Man Ohlman's backyard was even worse. It looked less like a lawn than a haunted forest. Three-foot weeds stretched from one rickety fence to the other.

"Yeesh," said Old Man Ohlman. "Good luck."

Hammie Rex and I got to work. Old Man Ohlman had an antique, motorless push mower. It was no use, though. The weeds were too thick. Instead he went inside and came back with a large, rusty pair of scissors. The sun beat down on us as I snipped away and Hammie Rex used his dino-strength to yank weeds, some of which were honestly full-on trees. Old Man Ohlman brought us two ice-cold glasses of "unsweetened lemonade," which was another way of saying lemon juice. I drank a few sips of mine to be polite but Hammie spat his all over the old patio we had accidentally uncovered. Around four p.m. we thought we made an incredibly important archaeological discovery but it just

turned out to be an old garden gnome mummy-wrapped in crabgrass. From the porch, Old Man Ohlman told us his name was "Dwayne" and that he had been banished long ago for disloyalty. By five o'clock we could actually push the lawnmower through the grass, and by six, the yard was looking perfectly clipped—a pure, orderly vision of conscientious suburban lawn care.

"Now that's a job well done," said Old Man Olhlman, beaming. "I see why they selected you as the world's first child astronaut."

"Yep," I said, panting. I was tired and sweaty and covered in bug bites and thorn pricks. I didn't have the energy to correct him.

"Time for your well-deserved payment, young fellow," said Old Man Ohlman. "Four dollars and twenty-seven cents!"

"What?" I said. "But we worked for five hours!"

"Ah, good point; $3.92 ought to do it then," said Old Man Ohlman. "Let me just grab the old penny jar." He disappeared and returned with a jar that was the size of a pygmy goat. Old Man Ohlman plunked it down on the ground and started to count out pennies. “I put a penny in this jar every time I don’t swear.” He dropped a penny in and then took it back out. “You know, you two are A-OK,” said Old Man Ohlman. “Unlike that traitorous blackguard Dwayne.” He shot the gnome a dirty look.

I was too exhausted to even argue. I just held out my hand and watched the pennies slowly (and I do mean slowly) pile up. Out of the corner of my eye I saw Hammie Rex’s whiskers twitch. His ears perked up. The little guy let out a whine.

“What is it, boy?” I said. “You hear something?”

“Has Augustine D. Katz, heir to the Katz dog grooming fortune, been kidnapped?” said Old Man Ohlman with a gasp. “To the Ohlman-mobile!”

Hammie shook his head, then snarled and bounded across Old Man Ohlman’s newly trimmed lawn. He stood beside the rickety backyard fence, making a low growl in the back of his throat. I caught up to him a second later.

“What’s going on?” I asked. “Is somebody spying on—”

On the other side of the fence, somebody ran.

CHAPTER 8

HAMMIE AND I burst out of Old Man Ohlman's backyard gate just in time to see someone disappear around the corner of the block. Whoever was spying on us had to be the same person who sent Gooboo the Snuzzle to commit oodles of homicide!

"Don't lose them, Hammie!" I cried.

Hamstersaurus Rex grunted and charged ahead after the mystery figure.

I caught up to the little guy a block and a half later. He stood at the trunk of a tall elm, growling. I peered up through the leaves. A large shape cowered on a low branch. Sure enough, there was a person up there—Hammie Rex had treed the spy!

"I'm putting you under Hamster Monitor arrest!" I said. "Come down with your hands up."

"Okay!" said the person in the tree. "Wait, what? How am I supposed to do that?"

"Good point," I said. "Come down first, using your hands, then put them up afterward. Two-step process. Got it?"

"Promise me Hamstersaurus Rex won't eat me!" said the spy.

"Probably won't happen," I said, "but I'm leaving all our options on the table."

"Okay, fine." The shadowy figure dropped out of the tree. It was Cid Wilkins.

"Hello, Sam," said Cid with a weak smile.

"Cid?!" I said. "What were you doing back there?"

"Look, I know that it may have

seemed suspicious but it wasn't!" said Cid. "I promise!"

Hamstersaurus Rex snarled and snapped his dino-jaws in Cid's general direction. Cid cringed.

"Uh-huh," I said. "So if not 'suspicious,' how would you describe peeking through a hole in the fence and then bolting the second we saw you?"

"Poor social skills?" said Cid. "Look, I live in this neighborhood and I happened to be walking by and I heard Hamstersaurus Rex and I wanted to say hi but . . ."

"But what?" I said.

"Well, I don't know," said Cid, staring at the ground and shuffling his feet. "I felt kind of intimidated because you're so cool!"

"Huh?" I said, looking behind me. "Who are you talking t— Wait, you mean me?"

"Of course!" said Cid. "You've had all these adventures and you can draw really well and you're super funny!"

"Hmm," I said. "Go on."

"Dude, you saved your whole school on multiple occasions," said Cid. "The most important thing I've ever saved is some wrapping paper, so it could be used again." He looked at his shoes. "It never was."

"Okay, yes, I did save the school," I said. "But there's no reason to feel intimidated because you think I'm . . . how exactly did you put it?"

"So cool," said Cid.

Needless to say, this was the first time I'd ever heard anything like this, and I realized I could get used to it.

"Right," I said. "Well, no worries then, Cid. Hammie and I have definitely done our fair share of sneaking. Occasionally past nine-foot-tall squirrels."

Cid looked relieved. "Hey, speaking of: as a fan I've just got to ask, when Squirrel Kong grew from normal squirrel size to giant squirrel size, how did that not violate the law of conservation of mass?"

"Uh," I said. "I guess just add that to the long list of laws Squirrel Kong broke?"

Cid burst out laughing. "Dude, you're *so* hilarious!" he said. "Anyway, I'm really sorry I spooked you two. Don't hold it against me. I guess I'll see you at school on Monday, Sam. Bye, Hammie." Cid gave a nod and started to walk away.

"Cid, wait," I said. "What are you up to right now?"

"Kind of embarrassing," said Cid. "I'm pretty friendless so I was just heading back to my house to play video games by myself. You're welcome to join—" He caught himself. "Not that you'd want to do that, necessarily! You are *the* Sam Gibbs. I'm sure you've probably got somewhere really awesome to be right now."

"Nope!" I said, probably too quickly. "I mean . . . I like video games."

"Neat," said Cid. "Well, anyway, my house is kind of lame or whatever, so apologies in advance."

Cid's house wasn't lame. And it wasn't a house so much as a small castle. Past a heavy-duty security gate set in a tall hedge, there was a three-story mansion surrounded by acres of lush greenery. I'd walked past this block many times and I had no idea this place even existed.

"Wow, you actually live here?" I said.

"Yeah," said Cid, shaking his head. "Sorry about the state of the topiary." Cid waved to the bushes on the lawn, which had been cut into the shapes of various fantastic animals. "The gardener was out sick this week. That elephant's starting to look more like a woolly mammoth!"

"Sure, I hate it when that happens to my topiary," I said.

Inside, Cid's house was no less impressive. I followed him through the front door, down a cavernous hallway. It was all paintings and chandeliers and sturdy-looking antique furniture. Most of the furniture at the Gibbs' residence had a folded and unfolded position.

"Want a soda?" said Cid, stopping at a sleek-looking stainless steel machine roughly the size of a refrigerator.

"Sure," I said. "Anything to get the unsweetened lemonade taste out of my mouth."

"What flavor do you want?" said Cid.

"Uh, I guess orange?" I said. My mom didn't let me drink soda at all and I was incredulous that some people had more than one type on hand. I guess this really was how the other half lived.

"Orange?" said Cid. "Sam, you can pick any flavor in the world. Go nuts, man."

"Then I'll take a raspberry and, uh, candy cane," I said.

"Now you're talking!" said Cid. He punched something into the machine's glowing digital keypad. I heard the sound of ice cubes plinking into a glass and liquid pouring. A few seconds later, the machine beeped and Cid took a tall glass of fizzy pink soda from a compartment in the bottom. He handed it to me. I took a sip.

"Delicious!" I said. "And kind of weird!"

Hammie yelped.

"If it's not too much trouble, maybe one for the little guy, too," I said. "It's easy to focus on how much Hammie loves to eat but, fun fact: he's often very thirsty, too."

"Wow, I feel like I'm really getting the inside scoop on mutant hamsters!" said Cid. "What flavor?"

"Hmm. Can this thing do chicken parm?" I said.

"Never tried," said Cid. "Only one way to find out!" Seconds later, Hammie's soda was done, too. I wasn't brave enough to taste it but it certainly smelled like chicken parm. The little guy drained his in a single long slurp and then gave a big toothy grin. It was nice to see Hamstersaurus Rex so relaxed, considering all his recent parental stress.

"Cid, I can't believe you have a machine in your house that can mix up any flavor of soda you want in thirty seconds!"

"Yeah. Sorry it's so slow," said Cid, punching in the combination for his own peanut-butter-and-pickle soda. "Maybe we should get the repair guy to come look at it. But he has to fly in from Denmark and it's a whole thing. Anyway, I figured we could drink them in the indoor skate park?"

"The what?" I said.

Sure enough, Cid had not misspoken. His basement had a huge custom-built skate park, complete with ramps and rails and half-pipes. Cid hopped onto his skateboard and showed us a bunch of tricks he'd invented. Pretty soon, Hamstersaurus Rex was out on a board skating around with him (the little guy was a natural!). Cid taught Hammie the "Elevator Pitch," the "Early Bird Special," and something he called "Fishing with Dynamite." Under his patient tutelage, I even managed to pull off a pretty good one-sixteenth-cab before the board shot out from under my feet and I nearly fractured my elbow. Still, just sitting on the edge of the ramp and watching Cid and Hammie Rex do jumps while enjoying a raspberry-and-candy-cane soda was pretty cool.

After that, we hit up the bowling alley, the climbing wall, and Cid's personal art studio.

"Check this out," said Cid. And he unveiled a painting he had done. It was a masterfully rendered scene of Hamstersaurus Rex, in full medieval armor, wading into battle. "I was really inspired by your *Swords of Hamstervalia* concept, so I threw a little paint on the canvas. I hope you don't hate it."

It was quite literally the most awesome thing I'd ever seen and I was speechless. Even Hamstersaurus Rex looked awed. His eyes were like saucers.

"Pretty . . . picture . . . ," I stammered.

"You get more vibrant color when you use oils, but I'm still such a noob, I stick to acrylics," said Cid, squinting at the canvas. "Sorry."

We left the studio and headed to Cid's game room. The floor was littered with awesome toys I'd never even seen before (Flubjubs! Zingo Spinners! You name it!). He even had several old-school arcade machines—Shark Punch, Alien Autopsy: Tournament Edition, and a rare imported copy of Ms. Super Plunger Jr. II: The Pipes, The Pipes Are Calling—and none of them cost any money to play! I'd already died twice in Farmfighter before I noticed the shiny black game console hooked up to a massive plasma screen. Cid sat on a comfy-looking couch nearby holding a controller with an impossible number of buttons.

"Want to try the Gamehouser APEX 900 Black?" said Cid.

I nearly did a raspberry-and-candy-cane spit take. "The APEX 900 Black isn't even supposed to be released for another six months!" I said. "How did you get this, Cid? Are you some sort of criminal?"

"Nah, I just have one of the prototypes. Sometimes my dad gets products in advance because of his job," said Cid. "No big deal."

"What's your dad's job and would he be interested in adopting me?" I said. "Under the circumstances I'm pretty sure my mom would understand."

"Oh, he's, like, an investor, I guess. He made a lot of money investing in those little cardboard thingies that can hold four coffee cups," said Cid. "Now he just kind of does it for fun."

"And as a result, you get free video games half a year before their release date?" I said.

"Well, sometimes the games have bugs," said Cid, with a frown.

"Yeah, that sounds really tough," I said. "Not sure how you manage."

Cid went to the cabinet and came back loaded down with bags of Funchos Flavor-Wedges. Many of their labels were in foreign languages. "Hey, do you think Hammie Rex would like some—"

Before Cid could finish his sentence, Hamstersaurus Rex did a quadruple somersault and landed at Cid's feet. His mouth fell open and he started drooling on Cid's (very stylish) sneakers.

"Well, the little guy used to have a bit of a problem with that particular snack food item," I said, reading one of the labels. "But it would be pretty cruel if I didn't let him at least try Steak Tartare et Escargot Flavor-Wedges."

Hammie Rex tore into the bag and began a feeding frenzy.

"My dad brings international Funchos back for me whenever he travels," said Cid. "Hey, it just dawned on me. Since SmilesCorp is out of business, I guess they won't be making them anymore, huh? These could be, like, the last Funchos on earth."

Hamstersaurus Rex froze with a look of utter terror on his little face. His whiskers stood on end. His lip quivered. I tried to change the subject as quickly as possible.

"Anyway, so your dad travels a lot to do his investing, then?" I said, looking around. Since arriving, I hadn't seen anyone else in the massive house.

"No, he mostly goes on vacations," said Cid. "He

and my stepmom are on vacation in the Azores right now."

"That's pretty cool," I said. "Or maybe not. I have no idea where that is."

"Me neither," said Cid, with a shrug. "But after the Azores, they're planning to pop in here for a day or two before they go spend a couple of weeks on the beach in the Maldives."

"Seems like all the best vacation spots are plural," I said.

"I guess so," said Cid. "Hey, you want to play a beta version of Penguin Flinger Quest Lord Adventures? It really expands the universe and mythology of the original game, where you just flung penguins at works of fine art."

"Sure thing," I said. "I just need to hit the bathroom first."

"No problem," said Cid. "It's down the hall, thirteenth door on the right."

I left Cid and Hammie (who had resumed scarfing Funchos; he was now working on a bag of Maple Syrup and Poutine Flavor-Wedges) and stepped out into the hallway. After walking what seemed to be a couple of miles, I finally came to the thirteenth door on the right, only to find a sign that read "DO NOT ENTER" in bold, black letters. Odd. I wondered if I'd counted wrong, but it was too long to walk back and check. Instead I shrugged and turned the knob.

A pale, red-haired man burst through the door. "What in the blazes are you doing?" he bellowed in a thick Scottish accent. "You're nae al-lowed in here! Nae allowed!"

With a wordless scream I turned and fled.

"You're nae alloooooooowed!" echoed after me.

I ran as fast as I could, back down the hallway . . . or, wait, was it a different hallway? Who was that man? Where was I? Did I just pass the same nice vase twice? Too many nice vases!

"Hey, watch it!" yelped a girl as I nearly flattened her.

"Whoa! Sorry!" I said, backing up.

It was Cid's little sister, Sarah, clutching her laptop.

"Um, what are you doing in my house?" said Sarah.

"Looking for the bathroom!" I said. "Is that terrifying Scottish man supposed to be here, too?"

Sarah rolled her eyes. "That's just Rupert."

"Rupert?"

"Rupert MacFarquhar. He's our male nanny," she said. "Our 'manny,' if you will. I won't. Anyway, he watches us when our dad is on vacation, i.e., always. I wanted them to hire someone else but of course Cid insisted."

"Whew. That's a relief," I said. "But what's the deal with the 'Do Not Enter' door?"

"Who cares? I still haven't even been in every room in this dumb house," said Sarah. "Nobody ever tells me what's going on around here or cares what I think!" And with that she burst into tears.

I had no idea what to do. "Um . . . Hmm . . . Maybe don't do that?" I said. Not particularly comforting. I stared at the pattern on the carpet. It looked like a very expensive pattern.

"I miss my old friends!" said Sarah. "This town is the worst!"

"Okay, Maple Bluffs might seem a little boring but it really isn't that bad," I said. "We've got a school, which you've been to, and a Flipburger, and . . ." My mind was blanking. "Oh, there's this, uh, really great museum with a lot of *fascinating* antique dolls . . ."

"It's not fair that we had to move here, just because Cid—"

"Hey!" said Cid, strolling toward us. "What are you two talking about?" He was stroking

Hamstersaurus Rex, who was gorging himself on a bag of Tropical Taro and Guava Flavor-Wedges.

"Hi, Cid," I said. "I was just trying to sell Sarah on all the amazing stuff we have here in Maple Bluffs. I almost forgot the duck pond! It's this pond *that's full of ducks*!"

"I'll be sure to let her know about that next time I see her," said Cid.

I turned just as Sarah disappeared into a doorway down the hall and slammed the door behind her.

"Yikes," I said. "She seems a little bummed out."

"She's always been moody," said Cid. "But if she's acting weird and shy, I'm pretty sure I know why."

"You do?"

"Of course," said Cid. "She's got a crush on you, man!"

I could feel the blood rushing to my ears and my face turning strawberry red. "That's not . . . I mean . . . I'm not . . . I don't think . . . ," I sputtered. "Naaaaah."

"Why not, Sam?" said Cid. "You're the coolest

kid in school!"

"Well, that's true," I said. Hamstersaurus Rex shot me a look. "But just FYI, maybe don't bring that up with any other sixth graders at Horace Hotwater. I wouldn't want them to get jealous of how cool I am."

"So humble," said Cid. "Did you manage to find the bathroom okay?"

"Not even close," I said. "How come you didn't tell me you have a manny?"

Cid laughed. "Ah, so you met Rupert? Quite a character, huh?"

"If by 'quite a character' you mean extremely frightening, then yes," I said. "I'm not exactly sure working with kids is the optimal career for that guy."

"Oh, Rupert's scary at first," said Cid, "but once you get to know him, he's merely deeply unsettling."

I laughed. Hamstersaurus Rex belched.

"So, I've got to ask," said Cid, "why were you doing yard work for that old guy in the tinfoil hat who I sometimes see lecturing trees?"

"Well, it's a long story . . . ," I said. "Let's just say I'm a wee bit short on cash at the moment."

"Hey, that's no good, Sam," said Cid. "How can your old buddy Cid help?"

I told Cid the story of our laughably pathetic attempt to catch the Chameleonkey. He admitted he had already watched Beefer's Epic Ninja 360-Degree Fail video online. But he was intrigued: this was a classic Hamstersaurus Rex adventure he could actually participate in. And somewhere along the way we started hatching a plan. . . .

CHAPTER 9

IT WAS SATURDAY morning once again, and the Maple Bluffs Flea Market was in full swing. The local bargain-hunters were out—examining dented panini presses, rifling through piles of tarnished souvenir spoons, haggling over the Baby President figurines they needed to finish their collection—in short, they were searching for the absolute lowest price on things nobody needs to begin with. Hamstersaurus Rex and I stood by a vendor selling used bath mats. (Business was slow.)

"Heya, Sam Dunk!" said Cid as he walked toward us. "Sam Dunk" was the awesome new nickname Cid had given me. It was much better than any previous nicknames I had been saddled with through the years. ("Sir Stinks-a-lot," first grade; "Stinkface," second grade; "The Incredible Stinking Stinkbag," grades three to five. Thanks for those, Beefer!)

"Check out this cool windup moose I just bought!" said Cid, and he tossed it to me.

"Whoa! I've had my eye on this thing for a while!" I wound up the moose and watched it do a little hula dance. "Glad it found a good home."

"You like it?" said Cid. "You can keep it, my man."

"Really?" I said. "Thanks, Cid!"

"How's it hangin', Homerun?" said Cid to Hamstersaurus Rex. "Homerun" was another top-notch nickname based on Hammie's initials (Hamstersaurus Rex: Homerun).

Hammie yipped with excitement as Cid stooped and extended his index finger to give him the world's tiniest high five.

"Got a little something for you, too, buddy." Cid reached in his knapsack and pulled out a bag of

Funchos Wunderbar Limburger und Weisswurst Flavor-Wedges. Hamstersaurus Rex's pupils dilated as he dug into the (artificial) flavors of Deutschland.

"So, are you ready to execute operation Invisible Monkey Catch?" I said.

"We *maybe* need a better name," said Cid.

"Yeah, it is a little on the nose, huh?" I said. "But there's no time for that now. We've got a Chameleonkey to nab."

"Man, I can't believe I'm going to help capture an escaped SmilesCorp mutant," said Cid, pumping his fist. "This is even more awesome than jetpacking through the Alps!"

"You've done that?" I said.

"Only a couple of times," said Cid. "I'm over it."

We made our way to Madame Karla's costume jewelry table. When she saw Hamstersaurus Rex and me, she gave an exaggerated harrumph.

"Some help you were, young man!" said Madame Karla. "That brooch the Chameleonkey absconded with was a one-of-a-kind showpiece!"

"There are three more of them right there,"

I said, pointing to a small pile of identical hamburger brooches on her table. "Anyway, we're totally capturing the Chameleonkey this time."

Madame Karla crinkled her nose. "Even without your other compatriots?" she asked. "Where's the boy from the 'Epic Ninja 360-Degree Fail' video?"

"Whoa, you saw it, too?" I said.

"Of course, who hasn't!" said Madame Karla. "The part where he bellows 'spinning ninja jump-climb maneuver!' before his grievous accident is most amusing."

"Well, there will be no failing ninjas today," I said.

"And what about the visored twins and the green-haired muckraker?" asked Madame Karla.

"Don't need them," I said. "Just the elite crew this time. I'm talking about the A-squad. Me, my new friend Cid, and my old friend who's a mutated hamster."

Cid waved. Hamstersaurus Rex grunted.

"Again, I harrumph, and with more gusto!" Madame Karla harrumphed louder. "Now, are you merely wasting my valuable time with false hopes of capturing that larcenous simian, or do you intend to buy something?"

"Oh, we intend to buy something," said Cid. "As many somethings as this will cover." He plunked a bill down on the table. I didn't see how much it was, but from the look on Madame Karla's face it was enough for quite a lot of fake jewelry.

"Now here's a young gentleman who appreciates his bijouterie!" said Madame Karla.

After filling a bag with gaudy baubles, we made our way to the edge of the flea market.

"The mistake we made last time was trying to capture the Chameleonkey in its natural habitat," I said. "This time we face the beast on our terms."

"This spot look good?" said Cid. We were standing in an empty swath of parking lot, hundreds of feet from the nearest climbable object that was taller than me.

"Yep," I said. "If the little thief wants any of our shiny objects, it's just going to have to walk here."

"Well then," said Cid. "Time for phase two of . . . Operation Condor's Wrath?"

"Man, you are so good at coming up with names!" I said.

"You really think so?" said Cid. "That means a lot coming from you. Not just anyone could have thought up 'Squirrel Kong'! So catchy."

"You like it?" I said. "I always kind of regretted not calling her 'Squirrellossus,' like 'squirrel' plus 'colossus.' A little more highbrow."

"Nah, you trusted your gut and that was the right decision," said Cid. "Shall we?"

I unfurled an old bedsheet and we dumped our sack of costume jewelry onto it. Plastic emeralds and glass sapphires glittered in the late morning sun.

"This looks like the perfect Chameleonkey bait," I said.

Meanwhile, Cid pulled a roll of heavy-duty fishing line out of his backpack. "This is the stuff my dad uses to fish for marlins off the Grenadines," said Cid.

"Great," I said. "Now we just need to string all this jewelry together into the world's largest, most tasteless necklace."

"Let's make Madame Karla proud," said Cid.

So Cid and I got to work, meticulously threading the fishing line through each piece. Soon we had all 286 items of "bijouterie" tied to the fishing line.

"I think we're ready," I said.

Cid and I took our spot, crouching behind a nearby trash can. Meanwhile Hamstersaurus Rex gave a little growl, then scurried under the bedsheet and made himself as flat as possible. The little guy could get pretty flat when he wanted to. I always admired that about him.

We waited. But it didn't take long.

"Hey," whispered Cid as he pointed. "Look at that."

I squinted toward the blanket and saw a fake ruby toe-ring twitch. A butterfly hat pin shifted. Then a tiara with a diamond the size of a doorknob slowly floated off the sheet.

"Now," said Cid.

I leveled my oversized slingshot. This time, instead of a pointy car, I'd loaded in a water balloon. The Chameleonkey was pretty far away, and merely a week ago, I probably wouldn't have been able to make the shot. But for the past five afternoons, I'd gone over to Cid's house to practice at his indoor archery range (of course he had one of those, right next to the indoor waterslide) to improve my oversized slingshot accuracy.

As I took aim, I tried to think of a cool action movie line. ". . . Hey, Chamelonkey," I said, "time to stop *crowning* around."

Cid looked confused.

". . . Because a tiara is like a small crown," I muttered.

"Oh, I get it!" said Cid. "Nice one, Sam Dunk! Hilarious as always."

I let fly. The balloon sailed through the air and—SPLOOSH—it was a perfect shot! I could suddenly see a very startled (and bizarre-looking) monkey-lizard creature wearing the doorknob tiara around its neck and dripping with acrylic paint. (Cid said he never used yellow ochre in any of his paintings, so he was happy to sacrifice a bunch of it for the mission.) The invisible monkey was invisible no more.

The Chameleonkey gave a panicked shriek and then took off back toward the flea market, still wearing the tiara like a loose collar. The fishing line (with all the sparkling fake jewelry attached) trailed behind it, and at the very end—securely tied to the line himself—was Hamstersaurus Rex! As the Chameleonkey ran, the little guy got yanked along behind it.

"Follow those mutants!" I cried.

Cid and I lit out after them. The Chameleonkey reached the edge of the flea market and sprang into the air. It grabbed on to a rack of extra-wide neckties and scurried over the top. A second later, Hamstersaurus Rex trailed behind, smacking into a hat stand and upending a box of socks along the way.

"Would you like to buy some bowling cards?" said the bowling memorabilia guy to a hapless passerby. "Check out this Mikey Mayfield rookie c—AAAAAAGH!"

He screamed as the Chameleonkey landed on top of his head, leaving a big splotch of yellow paint, and bounded off onto a nearby sun umbrella. Hamstersaurus Rex yelped as he flew after an instant later.

Cid and I tried our best to keep up. Even if we temporarily lost sight of the Chameleonkey, we could still see Hammie at the end of the sparkly fishing line, bouncing off tables and bins like a tiny water-skier. The chorus of startled screams and yellow paint tracks also marked a pretty clear path through the crowd.

At last, the Chameleonkey skittered up the exact same light pole where Beefer had pulled his Epic Ninja 360-Degree Fail. Hamstersaurus Rex dangled beneath the beast.

"Oh no! Looks like it's going to head for the trees again!" said Cid, pointing. A few hundred yards away were the same woods where the Chameleonkey had disappeared to last time.

"Paint or no paint, once the Chameleonkey makes it to those woods," I said, "it will be gone again for good."

Atop the light pole, the creature crouched to spring.

"Hammie, now!" I cried.

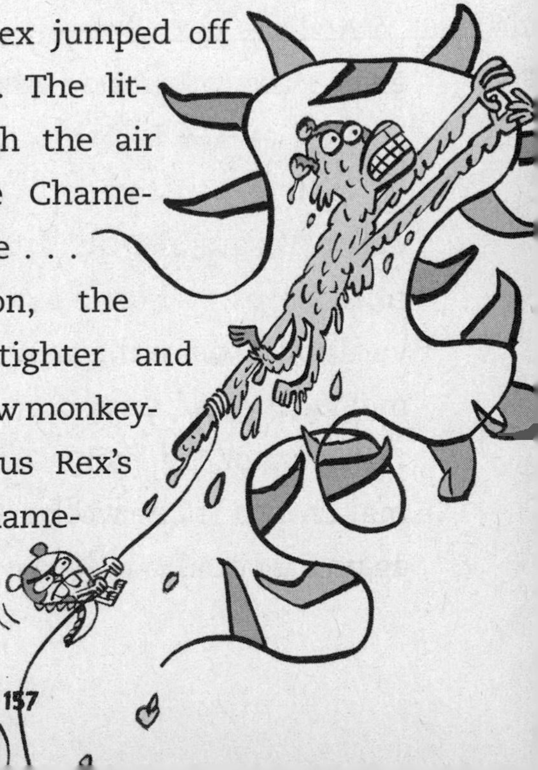

The Chameleonkey leaped and—KATHWANG! The fishing line snapped taut and the Chameleonkey froze in midair for a split second, before it was violently yanked backward by Hamstersaurus Rex, who clung to the pole with all his dino-might. The flailing Chameleonkey swung down in a wide arc and managed to grab on to a string of pennants decorating the tent of a festively painted gourd vendor. Before the creature could get its bearings, Hamstersaurus Rex jumped off the light pole himself. The little guy swung through the air and spun around the Chameleonkey, once . . . twice . . . With each revolution, the fishing line looped tighter and tighter around the yellow monkey-lizard. By Hamstersaurus Rex's eighth rotation, the Chameleonkey was tightly bound in fishing line, dripping yellow ochre onto the ground.

"We did it!" I cried.

Cid and I high-fived. A spontaneous cheer went up around us. I realized dozens of shoppers had watched the whole thing go down. The scourge of Maple Bluff's flea market had been captured. With the gourd vendor's permission, we cut down the pennant string. The Chameleonkey's strange reptilian eyes darted around in different directions and it nervously flicked a lizardy tongue.

"In you go!" said Cid, and he dropped the Chameleonkey into a newly purchased PETCATRAZ Plus™, the toughest medium animal cage on the market, and locked the cage door behind it.

"Bravo! You two lads and your faithful hamster companion truly are the champions of this alfresco bazaar!" said Madame Karla.

"Thank you, Madame Karla!" said Cid, with a bow.

"We couldn't have done it without your gaudy—I mean, stylish jewelry," I said.

"This time I do not harrumph but rather I huzzah!" said Madame Karla. "Huzzah!"

"Huzzah!" cried the crowd.

Hamstersaurus Rex beamed.

"Used bath mats for both of you!" said the lady selling used bath mats. "On the house."

"We're good," I said. "But thanks, though."

Truth be told, I didn't need a used bath mat to feel happy. It was awesome to finally rack up a win. And with Cid, I felt like I had an ally I could count on again (unlike some other folks I could name). The time was right to tell him about the Snuzzle. Maybe he could help me.

"Cid, there's something else that's been going on," I said. "Something that's a little bit more—"

HONK! I heard a car horn behind me. I turned to see that a sleek black luxury sedan was idling in the parking lot a few hundred feet away.

"Oh no!" said Cid, looking at his (cool, expensive) watch. "I've got to go! I'm grabbing lunch with my dad and my stepmom today before they go on their next vacation."

"Ah, okay," I said. "Tell them to enjoy the Maldives."

"That's where they just got back from," said

Cid. "They're headed to the Seychelles this time."

I was a little disappointed that I hadn't gotten to bring Cid into the fold and that we wouldn't be hanging out today. How exactly was I supposed to go back to my own toys after I'd been in the Wilkins' game room?

"Don't worry," said Cid. "I'll drop the Chameleonkey off at Maple Bluffs Animal Control on the way to the restaurant and collect the reward! Nice work, Sam Dunk."

"You too, pal!" I said.

"See you at school!" Cid hopped into the back seat carrying the Chameleonkey's cage and the car pulled away.

"Sam, where have you been?" cried Martha. She had appeared out of nowhere like some sort of most-likely-to-succeed jungle cat.

"Whoa!" I said, startled. "What? I've been here!"

"Well, I've been looking *everywhere* for you," said Martha. "I need to talk to you about something that is gravely important!"

CHAPTER 10

"ALL THE OTHER members of my Model Interplanetary Council delegation simultaneously quit on me!" said Martha.

"Your what now?" I said.

"Model Interplanetary Council," said Martha. "It's a competitive educational simulation where students learn about diplomacy by representing the planetary interests of fictional extraterrestrial species."

"Martha, in all honesty, that sounds like the nerdiest thing that has *ever* existed. And I say this as a kid who enjoys making dioramas."

"It is the nerdiest thing that ever existed!"

said Martha. "But that's not the point. The point is that without Dwight, Lucy, and Jimmy, we can't field a full four-person team. Which means Horace Hotwater will automatically forfeit. Which means I'll never become the first female nonconsecutive president." She squinted her eyes and gritted her teeth. "It'll probably be Caroline Moody instead."

I crossed my arms. "You know, I've been trying to get you to help me with something all week, but you couldn't spare a moment. Too busy to even take a look at the broken Snuzzle that—and this is going to sound really insignificant compared to Modern Interpersonal Planet People or whatever—tried to murder Hamstersaurus Rex!"

Hammie snorted in Martha's general direction and looked down his little nose.

Martha sighed. "If I'm being totally honest, I believed you could handle this one without me. It's not SmilesCorp or even a giant squirrel this time; just a malfunctioning toy. I thought you had it under control, Sam," she said. "Even though you often come across as cowardly and disorganized, you're actually quite brave and resourceful."

"Uh, thanks?" I said. "But I *don't* have this one under control."

"Then I guess I let you and Hammie Rex down," said Martha. "On the one hand, I'm a Hamster Monitor, the highest calling a sixth grader can answer." She reverently touched the Hamster Monitor patch ironed onto her sleeve. "On the other, I've got forty hours of e-curricks per week to manage because I'm trying to save a GPA that's in the toilet thanks to a nonsensical and frankly infuriating clerical error. It's hard to strike that balance. Sorry."

"Yeah, well, I appreciate the apology but I've got a lot on my plate right now, too," I said. "So, what is it that you want me to do exactly?"

"Well, I need you to join Model Interplanetary Council," said Martha.

"What?" I said. "Absolutely not! Just persuade your old teammates to come back."

Martha bit her lip. "I'm afraid that bridge has been burned," she said. "Once certain things are said, they can't be unsaid."

"What happened?" I said.

"They all claimed I was riding them too hard," said Martha, "but I merely observed that they're a bunch of weak, pathetic babies who don't have what it takes to win."

"Hoo boy," I said. "Well, I'm sorry they're all gone, but there's no way I can put in a ton of time on this right now."

"It's only for a week!" said Martha. "The competition is next Saturday. Dylan already said she's on board, too. Dylan is your best friend, Sam. And as I understand friendship, this should be a strong motivating factor for you, emotionally!"

"Yeah, well, Dylan hasn't been much of a 'best friend' lately," I said. "She's got other priorities. And I do, too. My main deal right now is figuring out who's gunning for the little guy."

"I can help you with that!" said Martha. "I usually don't say this, but I'm very, very smart!"

"You say that all the time," I said. "And on top of the Snuzzle mystery I'm still $624.25 in debt to Tenth Street Toys."

"Well, that's perfect!" said Martha. "Because if

we win Best Delegation at Model Interplanetary Council, there is a one-thousand-dollar prize. We're free to split it, and you can even have my share. I know you're not great at math but that's half the money!"

I wasn't great at math. But even I knew that five hundred dollars, plus my part of the Chameleonkey reward money, would be enough to pay back Mr. Lomax in full. In fact, it might be my only realistic prospect for getting enough cash within the week.

"Okay, because I'm your friend, I'll do it," I said, "on one condition."

"Anything!" said Martha.

"You need four people on the team, right?" I said. "Well, the fourth member of the Model Interplanetary Council delegation should be Cid Wilkins. He's smart. He's cool. He's great at nicknames. And he's even got a really fancy watch, if that helps."

Martha winced. "Perhaps I shouldn't have said 'anything,' because I hate to be imprecise," she said. "Dylan also had one condition. She said the fourth member of the team must be Drew McCoy."

"Oh, come on!" I said, throwing my hands up. "Drew McCoy is deadweight. Unless this is going to be a fedora opinions competition, that guy is totally useless."

"My hands are tied on this matter," said Martha. "But I still need your help, Sam. Please."

I sighed. "All right, fine," I said. "But you have to use that famous brain of yours to help me with my thing ASAP. I need to know who reprogrammed the evil Snuzzle and why."

"Sure, it's just a matter of taking a look at the code that runs it," said Martha. "This is where ten years of computer lessons ought to come in handy."

"Ten years?" I said. "But you're only twelve years old."

"Unfortunately, they wouldn't take anyone younger than twenty-four months, so I've kind of been playing catch-up ever since," said Martha. "Anyway, we're going to need a computer."

"I know just where to find one," I said.

"Welcome to the Maple Bluffs Public Library, young patron," said my mom in her professional librarian voice. "Or should I say 'Bunnybutt'?"

"Moo-oo-oooom!" I said. "I told you, if you insist on a nickname, please use 'Sam Dunk.' Anyway, this is Martha. She goes to my school and stuff."

"Of course I know Martha," said my mom. "Her Linear A Club meets here every Tuesday and Thursday. How's it going with the deciphering?"

"Very good, Patti," said Martha. "I feel like we're really close! We might crack it as early as next week. Then it's on to Cretan hieroglyphs."

"Glad to hear it," said my mom. "You just let me know if you need any more graph paper."

"You call my mom by her first name?" I said.

"I call all adults by their first name," said Martha. "You should try it sometime. It's exhilarating."

"Anyway, Mom," I said, "we need to use one of the computers in the computer room."

"Absolutely, Sam Dunk," said my mom. "You can use number sixteen. I'm just going to need to see that library card."

"Wait. Seriously?" I said.

"Just because you're my son doesn't mean

you're exempt from the rules," said my mom.

"I really like your mom," said Martha.

I pulled out my library card and my mom scanned it. "Oh, and this probably goes without saying, but be sure to keep it down," she said.

"I know how libraries work, Mom," I said.

She nodded and then sniffled. Thanks to Hamstersaurus Rex hiding in my backpack, her nose was already running. "Ugh. One of the patrons must have cats or something."

"Yep, that's the reason! Bye!" I said as I hurried Martha along toward computer carrel 16.

Once we were out of sight, I unzipped my backpack. Hamstersaurus Rex blinked in the bright fluorescent lighting. "Okay, buddy, I need you to stay in the bag and keep a low profile. Extra quiet," I said to Hamstersaurus Rex. "If you can do that, there's an extra frozen burrito for you at home. I'll even unfreeze it if you want."

He growled (quietly) in acknowledgment. There was a time when I couldn't count on Hamstersaurus Rex not to rampage. But he'd grown up a lot over the past school year. Perhaps becoming a parent and/or battling telepathic moles has that effect sometimes?

"Okay," said Martha, cracking her knuckles and taking the keyboard. "Let's see that Snuzzle."

I dumped the broken parts out onto the desk. Martha crinkled her nose.

"Wow. Hamstersaurus Rex sure did pulverize it, huh?" said Martha. "We could probably learn more if it wasn't broken into *quite* so many pieces."

"Gee, I'm really sorry we weren't gentler on the remorseless robot that was trying to kill us!"

"I accept your apology," said Martha.

I frowned. "Still no sarcasm, huh?" I said.

Martha shrugged. Then she tried her best to reassemble the Snuzzle by reattaching various wires to the badly dented computer processor at the core of the toy. When she was done, it still looked like someone had put a clock radio into a coonskin cap and run over it with a car, but at least all the parts were connected. The only recognizable features were the Snuzzle's reattached right paw and its eye, now a free-floating orb connected to the rest of it by a thin yellow wire.

"Luckily, these things come with a USB port," said Martha. "We should be able to connect it to the computer to figure out what's going inside this smartpet's proverbial head." She plugged a USB cable into the Snuzzle and attached the other end to computer number 16. Lines of code now appeared on-screen.

"Cool," I said. "What's it mean?"

"Shhh," said Martha as she studied the screen.

I started counting ceiling tiles.

"Wow," said Martha, 321 tiles later. "This Snuzzle has been expertly hacked. Whoever did it was able to completely disable the manual on/off switch."

"Oh yeah," I said. "I already found that out the hard way."

"Let's just comment out that code, then," said

Martha. At the beginning of a line of code, she typed two forward slashes. "And now we'll try a manual reset. With the Snuzzle reactivated, we should be able to learn more." Martha flicked the Snuzzle's switch off then on again. There was an odd crackling noise from its voice box. Then the Snuzzle's red eye began to faintly glow. An avalanche of code spilled onto the computer screen now.

"Here we go. This is the good stuff," said Martha. "Yep. Looks, like the hacker was able to take full control of everything. Like so."

She typed a command in and hit Enter. On the table, the Snuzzle's paw snapped closed like a bear trap.

"Any way to figure out who did it?" I said.

"Maybe," said Martha. "For one thing, the hacker took the time to autograph their work." She pointed to a line on the screen that read:

// CONGRATULATIONS! YOU GOT HACKED BY THE SAW <3

"The Saw?" I said. "So evil but, credit where credit is due, such a cool nickname. Almost Cid-worthy."

"I have to confess I never understood why people want nicknames so badly," said Martha. "You're only going to confuse teachers and authority figures by using them."

"I think you may have answered your own question," I said.

". . . ooooooOOOOOOOOOooo," moaned the Snuzzle's voice box.

"Whoa," I said. "How did you make it do that? I didn't see you type anything in."

"That's because I didn't," said Martha.

Martha clacked away at the keyboard. Just then her computer screen blinked and then went all . . . *weird.* Strange numbers, characters, and boxes flickered in a shifting pattern.

"What's happening?" I said. "Is it something good?"

"I have no idea, but no," said Martha. "I thought I disabled the malicious code but . . . The hacker must have hidden a self-installing virus somewhere in there."

"The Saw!" I said.

"Hey, you can't just crash when I'm halfway through my novel, you stupid machine!" cried the woman at the computer opposite from us.

"What happened to my résumé?" shrieked the man at computer carrel 11.

I looked up. Every computer in the computer room was now flashing the same bizarre pattern as ours. The other patrons were standing up, looking around, confused.

"It's trying to spread the virus, Martha," I said. "Shut it down! Now!"

"I can't," she said, still frantically typing. "I've somehow been blocked out . . . What the fiddle-fluffs?! Sugar britches!"

I yanked the USB cable out of the computer. Nothing happened. The computers were still going crazy.

"It still seems to be interfacing with the network wirelessly!" said Martha.

"oooo . . . OOOOOOO . . . ," moaned the pile of Snuzzle.

I reached for the off switch. But its scrabbling claw snapped at me and I yanked my hand back.

"Whoa!" I said.

"DESTWOY," said the broken Snuzzle.

CHAPTER 11

THE SNUZZLE LURCHED off the desk and onto the floor. Slowly, awkwardly, it started to drag itself toward us using its one functioning paw.

"Sam, what do we do?" cried Martha, backing away.

"I don't know! I can't get near the switch," I cried. "We need—"

With a furious snarl Hamstersaurus Rex landed right on top of the Snuzzle—CRUNCH! Hammie clamped his jaws onto the thing's paw and tore it right out of the socket with a loud mechanical ripping sound. The shapeless

Snuzzle-thing sparked and twitched uselessly. I dove for it and flicked the off switch, which thankfully still worked. The Snuzzle's voice box crackled and the glowing red eye went dead.

Martha's screen flickered one last time and returned to normal. I got to my feet and saw that everyone in the computer room was staring at us, mouths open.

". . . Technology, huh?" I said. "Sometimes it's good. Sometimes it's, uh, bad. And isn't that the paradox—"

"What on earth is going on back here?" said my mom, who burst into the room. "I've never heard such a racket in all my—ACHOOOOOO!" She let out a sneeze that sounded more like a controlled demolition. The noise of it echoed throughout the library, startling a whole story-time group.

"Sab, what are you thinking? You cab't have Habstersaurus Rex in here!" said my mom, her nose now dripping profusely, as she shooed us toward the exit. "I'b very, very disappointed in you! This is by blace of work!"

"I know, I know," I said. "I'm sorry, Mom. Sorry, everybody!" I stuffed what was left of the Snuzzle into my bag and made for the exit.

"I'd like to apologize on Sam's behalf, too, Patti," said Martha. "I'm happy to give your son a stern talking-to about the importance of rules, if you think it would help."

"Blease," said my mom, shaking her head and wiping her nose.

"Martha, come on!" I said.

Outside the library, we regrouped on a nearby bench.

"Sam, whoever the Saw is, their code is extremely impressive," said Martha. "They might even be, ahem . . . smarter than me."

I blinked. "Hearing that is somehow more chilling than the Snuzzle coming back to life and kill us," I said.

"Anyway," said Martha. "I'm happy to assist with this very important mystery in any way I can. But right now I need to head home. We're having beetloaf for dinner, if you'd like to join."

"Nah, I'm good," I said. My hands were still

shaking. I had no idea if I could keep a helping of "beetloaf" down.

"Your loss," said Martha. "Beets are an excellent source of manganese and you've always looked a little manganese-deficient to me."

"What's that supposed to mean?" I said.

"Nothing," said Martha. "See you tomorrow at five a.m."

"Wait," I said. "What?"

"Model Interplanetary Council practice, silly," said Martha. "This Sunday is our last day off from school before the competition next week and I want to make the most of it. This is a new team and you've all got to learn the ropes—parliamentary rules of order, points of personal privilege, optimal placard placement. The fun stuff!"

"I can't get up at five a.m.!" I said. "I've never been up at five a.m.! I'm not even sure five a.m. actually exists!"

"Sam, if we hope to get in a twelve-hour practice we simply must get an early start," said Martha.

"Twelve-hour practice?!" I said.

"Don't worry!" said Martha, putting a hand on

my shoulder. "There's a break."

"A break?" I said. "As in one single break? Martha, I'm not so sure about this."

Her eyes narrowed and her voice got intense. "Listen, Sam, you need to win Best Delegation at MIC as much as I do. Maybe more," said Martha as she poked me in the chest. "Trust me, if I could pull this thing off by myself, I would. But the rules say I can't. So I better have some *true competitors* on this team with me. I mean people who have the *fire* for space diplomacy deep down in their guts, *warriors* who thirst for the destruction of their enemies on the field of battle—in this case mock committee meetings with other sixth graders. In short, I want *champions* who will represent the history, culture, and planetary interests of Zoblorg VII with *pride* and *honor*! Now, are you in or out?"

"I don't even know what Zoblorg VII is," I said.

"It's our home planet," said Martha. "In or out, Sam!"

"All right! All right! I'm in!" I said, half terrified.

Martha's expression softened again. "Okeydoke!" she said. "See you tomorrow!" And she walked off.

"Oof. What have I gotten myself into?" I said.

Hamstersaurus Rex shook his little dino-head.

That night I tried to poke around online and figure out who the Saw might be. But I'm not particularly web savvy (this is kind of Serena's thing) and "Saw" is such a common search word that I didn't have much luck. I did end up watching a bunch of videos where talented amateurs play pop songs on the saw, though. So that was a good use of three hours.

My alarm clock went off in the middle of the night (technically 4:45 a.m.). I rolled out of bed and joylessly ate some cereal. Then my equally grumpy and confused mom drove me—periodically sneezing, because Hamstersaurus Rex was still snoozing inside my backpack—to Model Interplanetary Council practice. Martha had apparently secured the use of the Horace Hotwater gymnasium for the team's practices.

Dylan and Drew McCoy were already here, giggling together about some inside joke, apparently okay with the ludicrously early hour. This only made me more irritated.

"'Sup?" said Drew.

"I am. At five a.m." I put my bag down and slumped onto the first row of the bleachers. Nice bleachers, soft bleachers, good-for-a-nap bleachers . . .

"What Sam meant to say is 'good morning,' Drew," said Dylan.

"I wouldn't call it that," I said.

Before Dylan could respond or I could nod off, Martha entered from the opposite side of the gymnasium.

"Greetings, new Model Interplanetary Council delegates," she said. "Or as we say on Zoblorg VII: *Doh meefa, xeesotee! Zlorrrrk.*"

Martha bowed. We all stared at her.

". . . That's the standard planetary greeting," said Martha.

We all stared at her.

"On Zoblorg VII!" she said. "Every Model Interplanetary Council delegation is randomly assigned a planet to represent at the competition.

We've been assigned Zoblorg VII, also known as the 'Jewel of the Crab Nebula'—that's merely one of thousands of Zoblorgian fun facts we all must commit to memory in a deadly serious manner, before the competition next Saturday. Now, do you have any questions?"

"Yeah. Why are we in the gym?" I said, rubbing my eyes. "It smells like moldy basketballs in here."

"Well, Sam," said Martha. "I'd argue that the unpleasant smell is actually perfect because Zoblorg VII's main economic activity is collecting and processing other planets' refuse. Over forty-three percent of our planetary surface is devoted to waste management! The rest is lava."

"Hang on, we're from some sort of burning trash planet?" said Dylan. "Ew."

"No," said Martha. "The people of Zoblorg VII are *resourceful scavengers* who ingeniously *recycle* the trash of other, more wasteful galactic civilizations to create all manner of useful things, from construction materials to clothing and traditional jewelry!"

"So we . . . wear trash?" I said.

Martha furrowed her brow. "I think you guys are focusing on the wrong things."

"If I could make a suggestion," said Drew, "we should wear fedoras instead of trash."

"Fedoras are unknown on the world of Zoblorg VII," said Martha.

"You still didn't answer my question about the gym," I said. "The library has a couch where I could lie down."

"Gibbs, stop being a *zaglorff* and use your head!" yelled Coach Weekes. "You're practicing in the gym because I'm the head coach of this team!" He stood in the doorway to his office wearing pajamas and holding a steaming cup of herbal tea.

We all stared at him.

". . . Do you sleep at school, Coach?" I said.

"Huh? That's not the— Look, don't worry about that, okay, Gibbs," said Coach Weekes. "In fact, I want you to give me three laps around the gym, right now!"

I stood up. Martha shook her head. I sat back down. Coach Weekes shrugged.

"The rules require every Model Interplanetary Council Delegation to have a faculty coach," said Martha. "I figured Leslie would offer the least amount of interference in terms of how I run this team, which, to be perfectly frank, is with an iron fist."

"And I make an extra two hundred bucks this semester," said Coach Weekes. "Works out for everybody." He sipped his tea.

"So how exactly do we go about learning these thousands of made-up facts about our made-up planet?" asked Dylan.

"We have to study our official planetary information packets," said Martha.

She handed us each a thick, spiral-bound guidebook with the Model Interplanetary Council logo emblazoned on the cover. The books gave a not especially brief overview of the history, culture, and economy of the fictional planet of Zoblorg VII. For example, did you know the atmosphere of Zoblorg VII is 33 percent nitrogen? Or that in the year 11,459 B.Z., Xyxlorff the Heptarch got a brand-new *sklorff*? I didn't either, yet after learning these two exciting facts, somehow I instantly fell asleep.

"Sam!" cried Martha.

"Don't call me Bunnybutt!" I said as I snapped awake.

"What is the main export of Zoblorg VII?" she said.

I considered the question. "The main export," I said. "Is it, uh, . . . *sklorffs*?"

"No!" cried Martha. "Our world is forced to import over ninety percent of its *sklorffs*."

"Even I know that," said Drew.

"Oh, you did not," I said.

Dylan's eyes narrowed. "Yes, he did," she said.

"Everyone, repeat after me," said Martha. "The main export of our planet is space pasta."

"The main export of our planet is space pasta," we all repeated.

It went on like this all morning. Sifting through mountains of incomprehensible Zoblorg VII info and then getting ruthlessly drilled on it by Martha. I wasn't sure how much of it I was retaining . . . or what *sklorffs* were. After our single break, we moved on to a mock debate of the kind we would face at competition. Our topic was the adoption of Galactic Resolution 872.3, a proposed law that increased a sales tax on disposable bags to five *glorffs* apiece. Martha and I were supposed to argue the pro side and Drew and Dylan would argue the con. Coach Weekes kept score, while also flossing and doing a sudoku.

"I stand before you here today to say that there is literally nothing more important than Galactic Resolution 872.3!" said Martha. "The passage of this law is not only crucial to the prosperity and well-being of the people of Zoblorg VII, but quite literally to *everyone in the universe.*"

Martha paused dramatically. I nodded in

support. Martha mouthed the words "Sam, you go now." I shook my head emphatically. Martha nodded emphatically. I sighed.

". . . Hi. Yeah, so, nondisposable bags are good because you can, uh, use them again, instead of just throwing them away," I said. "And in the grand scheme of things, when you really get down to it, uh, five *sklorffs* isn't *that* much, right?"

Martha face-palmed. Dylan smiled. My time was up. Confused, I ceded the floor.

"My colleague says five *sklorffs* isn't that much," said Dylan, straightening her notes for effect. "Well, perhaps to him it isn't, but most of us don't just have fifty thousand *glorffs* lying around, which is the market price of one *sklorff*!" She laughed mirthlessly. Point scored.

"*Glorffs* are our money, not *sklorffs*, Sam," hissed Martha. "Get it right!"

"Sorry," I said, gritting my teeth. "No idea how I mixed those two up."

"But this merely illustrates the underlying problem with GR 872.3," said Dylan. "It is a tax that will disproportionately affect poor and middle-class space aliens, that only stands to benefit wealthy fat cats, like *Sam Gibbs*."

"Hey!" I said. "Am not."

"Face it: you're out of touch, Sam," said Coach Weekes.

"Aren't you supposed to be impartial?" I said.

"You know we didn't have much growing up," said Dylan. "My daddy was a simple trash-miner who struggled to put a plate of space pasta on the *plodnorff* for us every night. He depended upon people throwing away their disposable bags for his livelihood. A tax like this would have destroyed our family."

"Thank you for sharing that, Dylan," said Coach Weekes, who looked like he might tear up.

"It didn't even happen!" I said. "Her dad's a brand manager!"

"No talking during another delegate's time," said Coach Weekes. "Twenty-five-point penalty."

"You're sabotaging us, Sam!" said Martha.

"Doesn't Drew have to talk?" I said. "What about Drew?"

"Leave Drew out of this," said Dylan.

"Despite his attitude, Sam has a point," said Martha. "If we hope to win Best Delegation, all of us have to contribute."

"McCoy, your go," said Coach Weekes.

"'Sup?" said Drew.

"Okay, Drew," I said, crossing my arms. "I can't wait for you to wow us with your amazing grasp of this non-fedora-related topic!"

"You're being rude, Sam," said Dylan.

"Agreed," said Coach Weekes. "Fifteen-point penalty for rudeness."

"It's all good," said Drew, trying to calm her down. "I'm happy to orate." He cracked his knuckles, cleared his throat, and straightened his fedora. "So . . . what I'm kind of gathering is that we're all sort of pretending we're from another planet," said Drew. "Have I got that right?"

There was a moment of stunned silence. Martha looked horrified. Dylan looked angrier than I had ever seen her.

"Nailed it, Drew," I said.

"That's it, Sam!" said Dylan, leaping to her feet.

"I'm not going to put up with your awful attitude any longer. Martha, I'm doing this as a favor to you. But I won't stand for it."

"My awful attitude? *My awful attitude?*" I said. "My attitude is amazing!"

"No, it's not," said Martha, who had put her head down on the table.

"Sam, your problem is you think you're better than everyone, just 'cause you've got a new rich friend, Cid Wilkins!" said Dylan.

"Huh?" I said, dumbfounded. "That's not what's going on at all. You think you can forget about all your old friends because you've got a new boy-friend, Drew!"

Dylan turned scarlet, then mauve. "Drew is *not* my boyfriend!"

"'Sup," said Drew.

"Wow, feels like there's a lot going on here, so I think I'm just going to go do some online shopping while you guys work it all out," said Coach Weekes, standing up from his chair. "Negative-fifty-point penalty to Gibbs. Bye."

Martha leaped to her feet. "Friends! Friends!

My last Model Interplanetary Council team descended into anger and recriminations," she said. "I can't let that happen again."

"Well, I won't sit here and have my non-boyfriend, Drew, be disrespected by Sam," said Dylan, and she crossed her arms.

"Well, I won't even be on this team unless Drew starts pulling his weight," I said, and I crossed my arms.

"Oh, like you're doing any better, Sam!" said Dylan. "You didn't even know the difference between *sklorffs* and *glorffs*!"

"Those two words sound very similar!" I said.

"Do not," said Dylan.

"Are we all still pretending to be aliens and that's why you guys are fighting?" said Drew.

"Look, I know this is going to sound crazy," said Martha, "but what if we all took an unscheduled second break to cool off?"

"Perfect timing!" said Serena. We all turned to see her standing with Beefer in the doorway to the gym.

"Salivations, Martha," said Beefer. "How are you on this fine, vertiginous afternoon?"

"I'm racked with anxiety but also consumed with a burning desire to win at all costs. Thank you for asking, Kiefer," said Martha. "What are you two doing here? You don't go to this school."

"I'm glad!" said Beefer, looking around the gym. "I'd forgotten what a dump this place is."

"Horace Hotwater Middle School is my number-one favorite place in the world," said Martha.

"No, me too," said Beefer. "Me too. Definitely. I'm really digging the . . . cheese smell?"

"That's moldy basketballs," I said. "What's up?"

"Sam, I have something I thought you should know about," said Serena. "It might just break your mystery open."

"Far out," said Drew.

"Who are you again?" said Beefer.

"No time for that," I said. "What did you learn?"

"So, 'Epic Ninja 360-Degree Fail' got a ton of hits," said Serena.

"My lawyer told you to take the video down!" said Beefer.

"Michael Perkins isn't a lawyer," said Serena. "Anyway, I've pretty much been following Beefer around filming him in case he, uh, produces more content."

"You mean has another terrible accident and hurts himself?" I said.

"Yeah, basically," said Serena.

"Not gonna happen!" said Beefer. "That was the only time I ever messed up."

"How about when you knocked yourself out cold by hitting yourself in the head with a marble trophy?" I said.

"I have no memory of that," said Beefer. "And I'm not sure why."

"Whoa. Nobody got it on video, did they?" asked Serena.

"Unfortunately, no," I said. "So, you've been filming Beefer?"

"Yep," said Serena. "Mostly it's been pretty mind-numbing. He likes to sit around in his sweatpants eating Funchos and watching this movie where all these werewolves explode. It looks super fake."

"Uh, it's *several* movies where werewolves explode and it does *not* look super fake," said Beefer.

"And I also do very refined cultural-type stuff, too, Martha. Like, for example, I play the lute."

"Ugh. That's the most boring of all. Renaissance music is a snooze. You should listen to Mary and the Feet," said Serena. "It's got kind of a late sixties garage vibe but definitely with some EDM influences."

"I feel like we're getting off topic here," I said.

"Sorry," said Serena. "Anyway, this morning Beefer went into Harry's Health Food Hut to buy some rash ointment—"

"I was purchasing general health vitamins!" said Beefer.

"And I was there filming him in case he knocked something over, or something fell on his head, or maybe he electrocuted himself," said Serena, "when I happened to notice another customer was buying Dinoblast Powerpacker."

"The stuff that mutated Hamstersaurus Rex," I said. "But that's not exactly suspicious. I mean, if they sell it, somebody must be buying it, right?"

"I didn't get to the suspicious part yet," said Serena. "This person was buying up *all* the

Powerpacker in the entire store. Like, cases and cases of it."

I paused. "Who was it?"

Serena pulled out her phone. "This guy."

On the screen I saw a video of a pale man loading a shopping cart with all the remaining canisters of Dinoblast Powerpacker that were on the shelves. As he went to the register to pay, the camera panned up to his face. I swallowed. It was Cid's manny, Rupert.

CHAPTER 12

"DO YOU RECOGNIZE this red-haired weirdo?" said Serena.

"That's Rupert MacFarquhar," I said. "Cid's manny."

"*Of course* that kid Cid has an evil manny!" said Dylan.

"Hey, Rupert isn't necessarily evil," I said. "Maybe there's a good explanation for this whole thing."

"Oh, I'm sure there is," said Dylan. "The explanation is that Cid is a total creep who is up to no good."

"Dylan, even if Cid's manny is evil, you can't just put that on him!" I said. "Maybe Rupert is acting on his own!"

"Who's Cid?" said Serena.

"I think it's this guy," whispered Beefer, pointing a thumb in Drew's direction.

"'Sup?" said Drew, who hadn't been paying attention.

"Cid is this new kid that Sam loves so much 'cause he's loaded and Sam gets to use his indoor tennis court," said Dylan.

"He does *not* have an indoor tennis court! His tennis court is outside! And I don't even play tennis, I pretty much stick to the indoor archery range and the waterslide, thank you very much."

Everyone stared at me.

"Cid is actually a cool guy!" I said. "Martha, I'm really sorry but I need to cut practice short. I've got to go investigate this lead."

"But what about Model Interplanetary Council?" said Martha. "It's only six days away! We're not ready!"

"I don't know," I said with a shrug. "Maybe I can do, like, a double practice tomorrow or something to make it up?"

"We're already doing two double practices

tomorrow!" said Martha. "You'd have to do four quadruple practices!"

"Whatever. Martha, this is a code-red Hamster Monitor type deal," I said. "I'm leaving."

I could tell she wanted to argue but she stopped herself. ". . . You're right, Sam," she said. "Let me know if you need backup."

I nodded and snagged Hammie Rex before heading to Cid's house.

I buzzed at the heavy security gate and a second later it opened automatically to let me in.

"Heya, Homerun! What's up, Sam Dunk! How's it going, you two?" Cid stood in his front doorway, wearing an odd, bulky helmet with attached goggles. "Man, I was just going to call you. You've got to check out this new VR helmet my dad got for free. It's a simulation that makes it actually feel like you're eating toast." He flipped the helmet down and did a slow toast-eating motion, then laughed hysterically.

"Maybe next time, Cid," I said, stepping inside. I scanned the hallway. "Is Rupert anywhere around?"

"I don't think so," said Cid. "But then again, it's a big house. I just found out we have a solarium."

"Great," I said. "Would you mind if I asked you a couple of questions?"

"Sure," said Cid, "but I don't know what a solarium is either."

"No, not about that," I said. "About Rupert MacFarquhar."

Cid flipped his VR goggles up. "What's up?"

"Like, how much do you really know about him?"

Cid stroked his jaw. "Well, I know he's from a village seventy miles outside of Aberdeen, and he plays a ton of backgammon against himself. Gets really mad when he loses," said Cid. "Not a lot of people skills but he's an okay guy, I guess. One of the top three mannies I've ever had."

"Well, I saw the guy acting kind of suspiciously," I said. "He was buying up all the Dinoblast Powerpacker in Harry's Health Food Hut."

"Really?" said Cid. "If I've got my H. R. trivia straight, isn't that the stuff that mutated the little guy into the awesome rodent-dino hybrid we know and love?"

"Exactly," I said. "The key ingredient, PaleoGro, is also what the Mind Mole used to take away Hammie's dino-powers and turn him into a normal hamster. PaleoGro is dangerous stuff."

"Yikes," said Cid, scratching his head. "So you're wondering why Rupert would need so much of it."

"Look, it doesn't necessarily mean anything," I said. "But right now somebody is gunning for Hamstersaurus Rex and I have no idea who it is. I know your dad gets all these awesome toys and games in advance through his job. Did he somehow get you a Snuzzle before they were available in stores?"

Cid paused. ". . . Yeah, he totally did. He owns stock in Fundai so they send him free stuff sometimes. I got some pretty sweet glow-in-the-dark Astro-Robo footie pajamas, too."

"Look, this might sound crazy," I said. "But is there any chance that Rupert got his hands on your prerelease Snuzzle and somehow, I don't know . . . reprogrammed it to terminate Hamstersaurus Rex?"

"I don't *think* so. He mostly drives us places and makes sure there are enough yogurt cups in the house," said Cid. "But . . . I guess you can never be totally sure someone's not an evil mastermind."

"Do you recognize this?" I tossed my backpack on the floor and pulled out the shapeless, broken Snuzzle.

Cid cocked his head. "Is it . . . a fuzzy slipper full of garbage?"

"It's the Snuzzle that attacked me," I said.

"Mine doesn't look like that," said Cid. "Here, I'll show you."

He disappeared down the hall, leaving Hamstersaurus Rex and me alone in the cavernous hallway. A few minutes later, Cid came back holding a box. Inside it was a Snuzzle.

"Here's the one my dad got me," said Cid.

He tossed it to me. This model was apparently called "Bobbo," and it was brand-new, still in its original packaging. I breathed a sigh of relief.

"Wake up, Bobbo," said Cid.

Bobbo opened its yellow eyes and blinked in a too-cute way. "HEWWO, FWIEND," it said.

Hamstersaurus Rex snorted.

Cid shuddered. "I never even took this thing out of the box because it just seemed . . . irritating."

"I don't get the appeal either," I said. "But then again, one of these things has been trying to kill me for the past few weeks."

"If it'll make you feel better, you can check and make absolutely sure this one's not evil, too," said Cid.

"You wouldn't mind?" I said.

"Be my guest," said Cid. "In fact, you're free to interrogate any of my toys."

I squinted at the Snuzzle. "Hey, Bobbo, what's your, uh, primary object?"

"I WIKE TO PICK PWETTY DAFFODIWS," said Bobbo.

"And do you also want to destroy Hamstersaurus Rex?" I said. I waved Hamstersaurus Rex back and forth in front of the Snuzzle's eye sensors.

"HMMM," said Bobbo, regarding Hamstersaurus Rex. "CAN I GIVE YOU A WITTWE SMOOCH?"

The Snuzzle blinked again and puckered its strange rubbery lips. It was adorable and more than a little nauseating. Hammie recoiled.

"Okay, I've seen enough," I said. "Sorry to be so suspicious, Cid. A regular old annoying Snuzzle is way better than a murderous one."

"No worries, Sam Dunk," said Cid with a shrug. "Just another day in the life of a Hamster Monitor, right? You've got to pound the pavement, chase down every rumor, interpret clues, et cetera. So cool."

I felt myself blushing. "Honestly, Hamster Monitor is kind of just a made-up thing. We print our own ID cards," I said. "And when all is said and done, it's probably a good thing you don't have an evil manny."

"Nope, just an incredibly awkward one. But I sure wish I could have helped you wrap up your Snuzzle mystery like we solved the Case of the Chameleonkey." Cid looked a little embarrassed. "It is okay that I call it a 'case,' right?"

"Absolutely!" I said. "You could even call it a caper if you want."

"Caper! Even better! Speaking of which," said Cid. He reached into his pocket and pulled out a wad of cash. "The Maple Bluffs Animal Control reward money."

"Whoa!" I said. "But wait, this is the full three hundred dollars. You deserve half."

"No need," said Cid, waving me off. "I was just happy to get to participate in an adventure with my new buddy Sam Dunk and the world's coolest mutant hamster." He scratched Hammie Rex on the tip of his tail. Hammie gurgled.

"I can't let you do that, Cid. I wouldn't have been able to do it without you. The fair thing to do is to recognize my friend's contribution," I said, parroting Dylan's words.

"Trust me, Sam Dunk," said Cid. "I'm a twelve-year-old with his own indoor waterslide who's bored of jetpacking through the Alps. The last thing I need is any more money. You take it and pay back Tenth Street Toys."

"Are you . . . sure?" I said.

Cid grinned and nodded.

"Wow, thank you so much," I said. "I don't know what to say."

"Say you'll hang out and try this toast simulator!" said Cid, holding up the VR helmet. "After you beat the toast level, you can try muffins, crullers, and even focaccia."

"I'd love to," I said with a sigh. "But . . . I should probably get back to Model Interplanetary Council practice."

"What the what-what practice?" said Cid.

"Model Interplanetary Council is a competitive educational simulation where students . . ." I stopped myself. "You know, actually the easiest way to explain it is that it's a huge drag. But it's something I've got to do."

"Keeping your word. Much respect for that," said Cid. "It's what makes you such a good friend."

"Thanks, Cid," I said. "Mind if I use the bathroom on the way out?"

"Sure, you know the way," said Cid. "Thirteenth door on the right."

"How could I forget?" I said.

I walked down the long hallway and stopped. I found myself standing at the familiar door with the sign that read "DO NOT ENTER." I looked at Hamstersaurus Rex. The little guy looked back at me.

"I don't know, dude," I said. "Should we?"

He grunted in the affirmative. Hammie wanted to get to the bottom of this whole thing as much as I did. Even if Rupert hadn't reprogrammed Gooboo the Snuzzle, there was still something off about him.

I listened at the door and I heard nothing. Carefully I tried the handle. Locked. Hamstersaurus Rex pantomimed breaking it open with his head. It was a classic Hamstersaurus Rex move.

"Wait," I said. "We can't just knock down one of Cid's doors."

Hamstersaurus Rex whined and backed up a little farther. Then he looked at me, awaiting the go-ahead for a super-strong head butt.

"Is there any way you could use your dino-powers to, like, quietly pick the lock?" I said to Hamstersaurus Rex.

The little guy squinted at me.

"Sam, this still isn't the bathroom," said Cid, startling me.

"Sorry!" I said. "I was just—we were—I wanted to see what was behind this door. Just to make sure."

Cid stared at me for a moment with an unreadable expression. Then he smiled. "No problem, Sam Dunk," he said. He pulled a large key ring out of his pocket, found the right key, and unlocked it. The door slowly swung open. Beyond it lay a small, dusty room. Stacked against the wall were the dozens of canisters of Dinoblast Powerpacker that I'd seen Rupert purchase on the video. Otherwise it was totally empty. There wasn't any furniture or even a single picture on the wall. Cid flipped on a light.

"Sorry about the dust," said Cid.

"Is this all he keeps in here?" I said, looking around.

"Guess so," said Cid. "To be fair, it's hard to fill up a house this big. I could definitely imagine another waterslide going in this room."

"Can I help ye lads?" said Rupert, who stood silhouetted in the doorway behind us.

Hamstersaurus Rex growled.

"Uh," I said. "Sorry, Mr. MacFarquhar, I didn't mean to—"

"Hey, don't sneak up on us like that, R-Train!" said Cid, capping Rupert on the arm.

"Apologies, Master Wilkins," said Rupert, who gave a slight bow of the head.

"Look, Rupert, Sam Dunk has a question for you," said Cid. "Why in the world are you stockpiling Dinoblast Powerpacker?"

Rupert sucked at his teeth. "I cannae lie: I'm a wee bit of a fitness fanatic and I'm trying to increase my muscle mass. With SmilesCorp nae in business anymore, I figured I'd better snap up every canister I could, before it's too late."

"No offense," I said. "But you don't really look like a 'fitness fanatic.'"

"Aye, that's because I've just started," said

Rupert with an eerie smile. "You can consider this the 'before picture.'" Then he rolled his sleeve up and flexed his pale arm. It made a small muscle.

". . . Okay, well, good enough for me," said Cid with a shrug. "Keep pumping that iron, R-Train. You satisfied, Sam Dunk?"

"Yeah," I said, staring at the floor as we walked toward the exit.

"I know I can be a bit gruff at times," said Rupert, behind me. "I didnae mean to scare ye or your growling beastie. . . . Is that a wee hamster now?"

Hamstersaurus Rex glared at him.

"You're half right," I said, and I walked out the door.

Cid escorted me down the hallway to the front door.

"Have fun at school this week," said Cid. "Let me know if I miss anything important Mr. Copeland says about saving money by taking cruises during hurricane season."

"Wait, you're not going to be at school all week?" I said.

"Ugh, no," said Cid. "My dad is insisting on making the whole family go heli-skiing on these artificial islands off the coast of Japan until Friday. Even Rupert is coming with us. Super lame. Anyway, you said that Model Interplanetary Council thingy is happening next weekend?"

"Yeah," I said.

"Well, maybe I'll come out to root for Horace Hotwater!" said Cid. "It's either that or hang out at the Maple Bluffs Flea Market again. Because, you know, I don't have any friends."

"All right, see you Saturday, Cid," I said as I collected my backpack. "Though it will definitely be less exciting than the flea market."

"Until then, Sam Dunk," said Cid. "I'll try to bring you back some Japanese Funchos." He scratched Hammie's belly.

"Bye," I said.

As I crossed the mansion's expansive yard—the topiary was in much better condition now—there was one detail that kept sticking in my mind. The floor of Rupert's little room had dust on it, sure, but there were places that didn't. Places that looked like there had recently been furniture. And why did the door to an empty room have a "DO NOT ENTER" sign on it, anyway?

As the heavy security gate clanged behind me, Hamstersaurus Rex whined from inside my backpack.

"Yeah, dude, I kind of feel like something's not right, too," I said. "Rupert MacFarquhar makes my skin crawl."

Hammie whined again. I took a look. The little guy was holding a folded scrap of paper in his jaws.

"What is that?" I said.

I took the paper and unfolded it. While I'd left my backpack unattended, someone had slipped a note inside. In large, typewritten letters it read:

"HE'S A LIAR. DON'T TRUST HIM."

". . . Did Cid put this in my backpack?" I said to Hammie Rex.

The little guy gave a yip. I stopped on the sidewalk and turned

back toward Cid's mansion. Through the iron bars of the gate, I saw a lone figure standing on his front porch. Rupert MacFarquhar had his arms crossed. I kept on walking.

CHAPTER 13

I NEVER GOT AHOLD of Cid while he was on vacation. The school week passed in a blur of quadruple and sometimes quintuple MIC practices. Thankfully there were no more attacks on Hamstersaurus Rex or his family—curious that this corresponded with the same period of time that Rupert MacFarquhar was out of the country. But with my head a confusing soup of Zoblorg VII trivia and competition rules, I hadn't learned any more about who the mysterious hacker "the Saw" was either.

Saturday rolled around. The day of Model Interplanetary Council had come. The Horace

Hotwater Middle School delegation arrived in an old yellow school bus (which Martha insisted on calling an "interstellar transport vessel") at the SnoozeKing Suites Hotel and Conference Center out by the interstate. As we pulled into the parking lot (or "entered the atmosphere of Iota Horlogii b" as Martha would have it), Coach Weekes stood.

"Listen up," he said. "It's the day of the big game—"

"It's not a game," said Martha. "It's a simulated session of an extraplanetary governing body."

"Button it, Cherie," said Coach Weekes. "Point is, now's the time for one of my classic Coach Weekes pep talks. D'Amato knows what I'm talking about. This will really get you kids jazzed up for this planet doohickey today. Am I right, D'Amato?"

"Oh yeah, Coach!" said Dylan. "Do the one about the mighty wolf spirit that dwells within each of us. That one's super inspiring."

"Aw, come on!" said Coach Weekes, throwing his hands up. "You spoiled the pep talk ending!"

"Sorry," said Dylan.

"Thank you, Leslie, for almost delivering such

a stirring speech," said Martha. "May I address the delegation?"

"Okay. Fine," said Coach Weekes, dejected. "Who cares?"

"We've come a long way in the last week," said Martha. "Some of us have made, ahem, more progress than others."

"'Sup," said Drew.

Drew had been completely confused during every single practice. As recently as Friday, he indicated that he thought we were all going to be competing in some sort of swim meet. As far as I was concerned, he was still deadweight.

Martha continued. ". . . But we worked hard and the point is, we have a real shot at winning Best Delegation. As long as we can remember that we stand together, as a team."

"Tell that to Sam," said Dylan.

"Tell it to Dylan!" I said.

"I *just* told it to both of you," said Martha.

Dylan and I had been bickering the whole week and it was 100 percent Dylan's fault for always sticking up for Drew.

"In conclusion," said Martha, "my fellow Scavengers of Zoblorg VII, know that as your head delegate and basically the real coach of this team—"

"Hey!" said Coach Weekes.

"—I believe in each one of you," said Martha. "Now let's get out there and show these other schools what we're all about. On the count of three: *Glorzzzb!* One . . . two . . . three!"

"*Glorzzzb!*" we said in unison, though I'm not entirely sure why.

"All right, delegates: costumes on!" said Martha.

"Martha, do we really have to do this?" I said.

"How well we visually represent the planet and culture of Zoblorg VII is a crucial factor the judges consider when awarding Best Delegation," said Martha. "So suck it up and put your wobbly antennas on!"

"All right, all right," I said as I put a set of fuzzy antennas on my head. We also had to apply a thick coating of teal face paint and, perhaps most humiliatingly of all, don our "traditional Zoblorgian garments." This consisted of pieces of trash crudely stitched together. My outfit was an ill-fitting tunic made of an old soda box sewn to a garbage bag with some dental floss. I completed my ensemble with a necklace of crushed cans.

"So . . . how do I look?" I said to Hammie Rex as I dabbed the last of the greasepaint around my eyes. Hamsters can't really laugh, but he sure looked like he wanted to.

Annoyingly, Dylan and Drew seemed to actually enjoy dressing up as Zoblorgians. They were cooing over each other's matching outfits: trash "sweaters" made of shower curtains and scarves of old inner tubes.

As head delegate, Martha wore a shiny, inside-out Funchos bag on her head and carried a traditional Zoblorgian "Scepter of Authority" that was actually a broken smoke alarm taped to a broomstick.

Even Coach Weekes was not exempt from the costuming requirement. He grudgingly applied some face paint and put on a tank top made of old newspapers.

Once we looked like five space aliens who hailed from a burning trash planet in the Crab Nebula, we crossed the parking lot of the SnoozeKing Suites Hotel and Conference Center to check in.

"Wow, look at all these little weirdos," said Coach Weekes.

The lobby was filled with other kids and their coaches, dressed like their assigned alien species. The delegation from Oak Cliffs Middle School was painted gold like the Automata of Excelsion Prime.

EXCELSION PRIME

The team from L. L. Dupree were shrouded in dirty bandages as the Grub People

of Third Moon of Biplos. I gave an involuntary shudder as I saw that every third kid at Model Interplanetary Council seemed to be clutching a Snuzzle. Omar wasn't kidding: they truly were the hottest toy of the spring season.

A woman in a shimmering robe with a high pointy collar sat at a table with the MIC sign-in sheet, looking bored.

"*Doh meefa, xeesotee! Zlorrrrk*," said Martha with a bow.

"Sure," said the woman, who seemed like she'd already heard quite a few traditional alien greetings this morning. "Team name and home planet?"

"Horace Hotwater Middle School; Zoblorg VII," said Martha.

The woman checked us off her list. "Please go

to the Chamber of Unity, that's Conference Room B, for the Galactic Invocation Ceremony," she said.

Nearby, a coach—made up to look like a bald gray alien—seemed to be staring at me. Somehow he looked incredibly familiar, yet I couldn't quite place him. Before I could get a better look, he melted back into the crowd, perhaps to rejoin his team.

"Follow me," said Martha. "I memorized the layout of the SnoozeKing Suites in advance so I could plot the shortest routes between rooms."

We quickly made our way to a large hotel conference room filled with hundreds of middle school alien delegates. They all sat at tables arranged in semicircular rings in front of an elevated dais. Hanging above us was a gigantic mobile model of the Milky Way galaxy. Even I had to admit, the whole scene was as impressive as it was nerdy.

"This is us," said Martha, proudly pointing to a placard that said "Zoblorg VII" with four empty seats behind it.

"Good luck, kids," said Coach Weekes.

"Remember: you can't spell 'succeed' with 'u' and 'me.'"

By the time I'd realized that wasn't true, he'd already taken his seat in the small section at the back with the other coaches and pulled out his sudoku book.

"Wow, so . . . are all the other kids, like, pretending to be aliens, too?" said Drew.

"Very insightful," I said. "You're really starting to put it all together, Drew. I'm so proud of—"

"Stow it, Sam," said Dylan. "The ceremony is starting. You're being rude."

Up on the dais, a girl with thick glasses and bunch of extra eyes glued to her face had taken the podium. She loudly banged a crystal against a geode, until the assembly quieted down.

"Greetings, planetary delegates!" said the girl. "I hereby call this session of the Model Interplanetary Council to order!"

A cheer went up.

"That's Galactic Consul General Fatima Jabour from Kepler 10b / Isaac Newton Magnet School for Science," whispered Martha. "Fatima's an

MIC legend—leader of last year's Best Delegation and fairly strong competition for first female nonconsecutive president. She's the one who decides which delegations are assigned to what committees."

"Cool," I whispered. "What?"

"Ha!" said Dylan. "Now who doesn't know what's going on?"

"I'm playing dumb for Drew's benefit!" I said. "I figured he'd be too embarrassed to ask."

"'Sup," said Drew.

"Shhh!" said Martha. "If we get a juicy assignment, like, say, the Death Ray Disarmament Committee, it'll be much easier for us to win Best Delegation. We just don't want something boring like the Committee to Prevent Relativistic Accounting Mistakes or the Committee on Spaceship Furniture Safety."

Fatima Jabour continued. "I will now announce the delegations assigned to the Committee to End Robot Exploitation," she said, reading off a list. "The Bird-lords of Somnus II, The Muscle-oids of Herculon, The Sentient Treefolk of Planetoid X . . ."

My mind wandered a bit as the Consul General went through all the committees and the delegations assigned to each. Something so familiar about that gray alien coach . . .

"Come on, Death Ray Disarmament . . . come on, Death Ray Disarmament . . . ," Martha muttered under her breath the whole time.

In the end, the Scavengers of Zoblorg VII were not assigned to the Death Ray Disarmament Committee. Instead we got the Committee for the Preservation of Space Fungus.

". . . Is that a good committee?" I whispered to Martha.

She rubbed her temples. "No, Sam. It's the only one worse than Accounting Mistakes." She took a deep breath and an instant later she was cheerful again. "It's okay, though. We can do this. An obstacle is just an opportunity! An obstaclunity! Just like my unfair GPA error! All we have to do is work twice as hard and make zero mistakes!" Martha's smile had gone from chipper to slightly insane.

As the delegates filed out of Conference Room B / the Chamber of Unity to reconvene in their smaller committees, someone in the crowd tapped me on the shoulder. I turned to see Cid Wilkins.

"Sam Dunk!" said Cid. "I came straight from the airport to support the team! Go Horace Hotwater!"

"Cid, I've got to talk to you," I said. "There was a—"

"Glad to see you, lad," said Rupert MacFarquhar, who loomed over Cid, looking as creepy as ever. "Quite a colorful extracurricular you kiddies do here in the States. Where I'm from it was rugby union, caber toss, or nothing."

I felt Hamstersaurus Rex moving inside my bag, agitated at the sound of Rupert's voice. I tried to calm the little guy down.

"Sam, you were saying something," said Cid. "There was a . . . what?"

"Oh yeah. There was a . . . parking ticket," I said. "On your car! Outside!"

"My car? But the spot was unmarked," cried Rupert. "I dinnae park illegally, I swear by the stones of Dumbarton Castle!"

I shrugged. "I don't know," I said. "It looked like they might tow it."

"Ach! No tow!" cried Rupert, and he ran for the exit. "No tow!"

"Wow, thanks for looking out," said Cid.

"Cid, I need to ask you something," I said.

"If you want to know about the heli-skiing, honestly, it was a total snooze," said Cid. "If you've dropped out of a helicopter and skied down a dormant volcano once, you've done it a million times."

"No, not your vacation," I said. "I want to ask you about the note you put in my backpack! What is Rupert lying about? Is he dangerous?"

"Note?" said Cid. "What note?" He seemed genuinely confused.

"The note that . . . ah, never mind," I said. "I must have gotten mixed up. Sorry." Before I had time to process the implications of this, Dylan grabbed my arm.

"Sam, what's taking you so long!" said Dylan. I realized the rest of the team had left me behind and she'd been sent back to collect me. She noticed Cid. "Oh, sorry, didn't realize you were hanging out with your new best friend."

"Cid's not my new best friend," I said.

Cid looked taken aback.

"I mean, he's obviously my best *new* friend," I said. "But I don't have any other new friends."

"Greetings, m'lord Cid," said Dylan with a bow. "We've met before but I'm just a peasant, so no sweat if you don't remember my name. It's Dylan, by the way. Sam and I used to hang out."

"Uh. Hi," said Cid. "Of course I remember."

"Dylan, stop!" I said.

"So sorry to embarrass you in front of the aristocracy, Sam," said Dylan. "But it's time to go. I don't want us to lose Best Delegation because *you're* late."

"I'm really sorry about this, Cid," I said. "I'll talk to you later."

"Sure, no problem," said Cid, who still looked quite puzzled and uncomfortable. "Bye, Sam."

"That was really rude back there!" I whispered to Dylan, once we'd gotten out of Cid's earshot.

"Yeah, well, that was just a taste of what you've been sending Drew's way all week," said Dylan.

"All those times I ripped on Drew I was just joking!" I said, which wasn't really true. "What? Can

Drew not take a joke? Another way he's lame."

"Sam, I don't want to argue about this right now," said Dylan, "but I will—"

We'd caught up to the other two Scavengers of Zoblorg VII. Martha looked impatient.

"Hurry!" said Martha. "Committee roll call is happening at nine thirty!"

Our team quickly made its way down the crowded hallway—past an alarming number of kids with their Snuzzles—toward Conference Room 2H, where the Committee to Preserve Space Fungus was supposed to meet.

Drew pointed at the team from L. L. Dupree (the Grub People of the Third Moon of Biplos), who were also on our committee.

"L. L. Dupree," said Drew, shaking his head. "Man, I hate those guys."

"Drew, you know it's just a mindless, arbitrary rivalry," I said. "There's no reason for Horace Hotwater kids to dislike L. L. Dupree kids. It's all completely made up."

"You're made up," said Dylan.

"What does that even mean?" I said.

"Stop it, both of you," hissed Martha. "There are judges everywhere. Look!"

She nodded toward three stern-looking adults conferring in a nearby doorway. They had the telltale shimmery robes and clipboards of official MIC staff. Dylan and I (reluctantly) shut up.

"Okay," said Martha, talking quietly as we walked. "We have about forty-five seconds to talk strategy: we need to decide if Zoblorg VII is for or against the preservation of space fungus."

"Huh? I didn't even know that was a question. Isn't it the Committee *for* the Preservation of Space Fungus?" I said. "Why would we be against it?"

"It's risky," said Martha, "but it gives us the opportunity to make a flashy, controversial argument and really stand out from the crowd. If executed well, MIC judges will eat it up."

"Hmm. I like it," I said. "Plus, if I'm being honest, space fungus sounds pretty gross. Yeah. Let's be against it."

"I strongly believe we should be *for* preserving it," said Dylan, crossing her arms. "Space fungus is just as important as any other endangered species. Like tigers or whales."

"You're just saying that 'cause it's the opposite of what I said!"

"Am not," said Dylan.

"Martha, she's doing it again!" I said.

"Shhh," said Martha. We had arrived at Conference Room 2H. "I'm not sure what the right choice is. Play it safe or take a chance?" said Martha, sucking at her teeth. "I'll know when the time is right. Just pay close attention and follow my lead. On three: *Glorzzzb*. One, two, three . . ."

"*Glorzzzb*," we all whispered.

The Zoblorg VII delegation found our seats at one of several smaller tables. Soon every chair in the room had been filled. A boy sitting at the front—made up to look like some sort of purple reptile creature—banged a smaller crystal against a smaller geode.

PURPLE REPTILE CREATURE FROM FLARGOXX

"Greetings, delegates, I am Committee Grand Archon Dave Cunningham from Flargoxx the Shadow Planet / Ives McGaffney Middle School," he said. "I hereby call the Committee for the Preservation of Space Fungus to order. I now move to hear any motions presented by the delegations. Raise your placard to introduce a motion."

Several delegates held their placards up. Martha didn't. It was unlike her not to raise a hand. I guess she was still mulling our team strategy. The Grand Archon scanned the room.

"The committee recognizes the delegation from the Third Moon of Biplos," said the Grand Archon.

"*Glomby gomby gleeeeeglob!*" said the L. L. Dupree team in unison. Then a kid with a bowl cut took the lead. "That is the traditional Grub Person greeting that you might hear in the warm, habitable tunnels beneath the frozen, nightmarish surface of our world. This delegation would like to make a motion affirming that the discussion of the preservation of space fungus is a really neat thing to do."

"Noted. All in favor, raise your placards," said the Grand Archon.

All the committee delegates raised their placards.

"All opposed, raise your placards," said the Grand Archon.

No one raised any placards.

"Let the record show that the committee affirms that the discussion of the preservation of space fungus is a really neat thing to do," said the Grand Archon.

This was the gist of Model Interplanetary Council, a bunch of boring stuff governed by a lot more super-boring rules. Even when it wasn't happening at five a.m. it was hard to stay awake. I tried my best as countless motions, points of personal privilege, seconds, and waivers were introduced and voted on. The experience actually made me long for Mr. Copeland's cruise-ship tips. Inside my bag, I heard Hamstersaurus Rex quietly snoring. I unzipped it a few inches. The little guy looked so peaceful. Oh how I wanted to join him . . .

"The committee recognizes the Scavengers of

Zoblorg VII," said the Grand Archon.

Martha stood.

"*Doh meefa, xeesotee! Zlorrrrk,*" said Martha. "We stand in this committee today to represent the world of Zoblorg VII, a proud lava-covered planet with a long and complicated history that I will now tell you about. . . ."

Martha spoke at length, and yes, I will admit, I stopped paying attention somewhere in the Zoblorgian stone age. My mind was racing. If Cid hadn't left the note, then who had? I'd been assuming the mysterious note was trying to warn me about Rupert, but . . . what if it wasn't? And who was the Saw anyway? They had to be connected. . . .

". . . and with that, I turn the floor over to my fellow Zoblorgian delegate, who can further elaborate on the subject," said Martha. "Sam." She smiled, tapped her Scepter of Authority on the floor, and motioned for me to stand up.

I slowly rose. While I was mulling over the Snuzzle mystery, I'd missed whether Martha had come out for or against the preservation of space fungus. The eyes of a dozen alien delegations were on me now, and I had no way to figure out the answer. Still, I had to say something. I looked at Martha for any clue as to which way she'd gone. She smiled blandly, though her eyes looked intense. I glanced at Dylan. She scowled at me. I looked at Drew. He was retying his inner tube scarf more jauntily.

"Yeah, so, our team, um . . . hates space fungus," I said.

A shocked hush fell over the room. I guess it really *was* a controversial argument.

"But this is the *Committee for the Preservation of* Space Fungus," said the Grand Archon, looking dismayed.

I shrugged.

"And that's actually what we want to do!" said Dylan, elbowing her way in front of me. "Please excuse my colleague for misspeaking so stupidly. He's probably our worst delegate."

I glared at her. "I didn't misspeak. And I'm not the worst delegate. The worst delegate's name rhymes with 'shoe,'" I said. "In fact, the planet of Zoblorg VII hereby declares war on all space fungus!"

"No, we don't! We vow to devote our entire GDP to saving space fungus!" said Dylan, glaring back at me. "Save the space fungus! Save the space fungus! C'mon, everybody! Save the—"

"Excuse me, Grand Archon," said Martha, clacking her Scepter of Authority against the floor. "The Scavengers of Zoblorg VII would respectfully like to introduce a motion for an emergency five-minute recess."

A murmur went up among the other delegations of the committee. The Grand Archon furrowed his brow. "Why?" he said.

"Because, uh . . ." Martha was stumped.

"I've got to go to the bathroom," said Drew. Whether it was quick thinking or just something that popped into his head, I had no idea.

"Okay, sure," said Grand Archon Dave Cunningham, looking a little embarrassed. "All those in favor of an emergency recess, raise your placards."

Somehow, we narrowly won this vote. Maybe there were other kids who had to go to the bathroom, too? Or maybe they collectively decided to take pity on the imploding team from Horace Hotwater? I grabbed my backpack as Martha hurried the rest of us out of Conference Room 2H. Drew made a beeline for the bathroom—his diversion wasn't just a clever ruse—while Martha marched us down the hall and around the corner to an empty hotel ballroom. She shut the door behind us.

"Wow. Nice work, Sam," said Dylan. "You probably cost us Best Delegation."

"Me? You're the one who started the fight!" I said. "You called me stupid!"

"No, I didn't," said Dylan. "I said you did something *stupidly*. There's a huge difference, and if you think that's the same as calling you stupid, then you really are stupid."

Martha cleared her throat.

"Sam, Dylan," said Martha, "WILL BOTH OF YOU PLEASE SHUT UP!"

Dylan and I went silent. Hamstersaurus Rex poked his head out of my backpack with a startled grunt.

"Sam, when I asked you to 'elaborate,' I wanted you to elaborate on Zoblorg VII's environmentally conscious way of life," said Martha.

"Oops," I said.

"See?" said Dylan. "I was right. He wasn't even paying attention!"

"Yes. But after Sam took his position," said Martha, "it was your job to back him up. Not get into an argument with him in front of the judges."

"But . . ." Dylan trailed off. Now she looked deflated, too.

Martha looked off into the distance. Then she began to speak. "Some say the natural order of the universe is chaos. That strife and conflict are the only constants out in the cold void of space. In the year 13,824 B.Z., the Interplanetary Council was formed to refute that dark proposition. The people of many worlds voluntarily came together because they believed that different species might put aside their quarrels and avert war through structured diplomacy. In short, this whole endeavor is about cooperation. Now I ask, if a hundred alien races can come together and peacefully hash out their differences, can't two best friends do the same?"

Dylan and I both stared at the floor now. We nodded.

"Excellent," said Martha. "Hamstersaurus Rex and I are going to wait here while you and Dylan find somewhere private. You have"—she checked her watch—"four minutes and eleven seconds to work out all your problems. After that, we're going to go back into committee and prove that we, the Scavengers of Zoblorg VII, are the best cooperators in the entire universe. In fact, we're going to completely destroy everyone else at cooperation. Got it?"

We nodded again. I handed my backpack to Martha and Dylan and I found a nearby supply closet. We stepped inside.

"Well . . . ," said Dylan.

"Well . . . ," I said.

There was a long moment of uncomfortable silence.

"Look, I'm sorry," I said. "I've been way too hard on Drew. He's not a bad guy. If I'm honest, I think I'm—I'm probably jealous of him."

"What?" said Dylan. "Why?"

"I don't know. Because you want to spend all your free time with him and go to disc golf camp and wear your matching scarves and stuff," I said. "I can't help but feel like . . . you don't even want to be friends with me anymore."

"Of course I want to be friends with you, Sam!" said Dylan. "I thought you didn't want to be friends with me."

"Huh? You mean because of Cid Wilkins?" I said. "Look, Cid's cool and I'm glad I met him, but I only started hanging out with the guy because everyone else was so focused on their own problems."

Dylan sighed. "It's not just Cid," she said. "Your real best friend is someone else now: Hamstersaurus Rex. I used to be the strong one; the one who was always looking out for you. And don't get me wrong, I love Hammie, but ever since he came along . . . well, you don't really need me for that."

"What are you even talking about? You've saved Hammie and me so many times I've lost count!" I said. "You helped stop Squirrel Kong and the Mind Mole! Your golf disc is what prevented Michael Perkins from eating Hammie Rex at Science Night. Both of us need you. A lot."

"You really mean that?" said Dylan.

"Yeah!"

"I guess it is kind of ridiculous to be jealous of a class pet," said Dylan. "Sorry I've been giving you a hard time, too."

"Look," I said, "maybe as we get older, the stuff we're interested in is going to change. The people we hang out with might change. And maybe our friendship will have to change, too. It's going to take some work to keep it together. But it's worth it to have a best friend like you."

"I feel the same way," said Dylan. "Thanks, Sam."

We hugged. Just then, the lights flickered and went out. A second later they came back on.

"What was that?" said Dylan.

We cautiously stepped out of the supply closet and made our way back to Martha. She was distracted, feeding Hamstersaurus Rex dried beet chips and attempting to teach him facts about Zoblorg VII. Meanwhile Drew had returned from the bathroom and he was rummaging through my backpack. The lights flickered again.

"Drew, what are you doing?" I said.

"Sam! 'Sup? Sorry. I smudged my alien face paint, so I borrowed some of yours." He held up the little tin of teal greasepaint.

"I told him it was okay," said Martha. "Makeup blotchiness is definitely a factor the judges consider. Some people say it's why Marneyville Middle School lost out on Best Delegation last year."

"Also, Sam, this is a rad Zoblorgian junk amulet you had in your backpack," said Drew. "If you're not going to wear it, do you I mind if I do? It even lights up!" He held up the remnants of the broken Snuzzle; its red eye was glowing.

"Drew, no!" I cried.

The Snuzzle's broken voice box let out a single crackly word: ". . . DES . . . TWOY."

"Turn it off," said Martha. "Now!" She snatched the Snuzzle away and flicked the off switch. Its red eye went dead.

“What’s going on?” said Dylan. “Why is everyone so—”

“DEWSTOY.” The word was repeated faintly. But it hadn’t come from the broken Snuzzle; it had come from outside the conference room door. We all looked at one another.

A thump came at the door. Then another. Then another.

CHAPTER 14

THUMP! THE BALLROOM door shuddered on its hinges. I grabbed a chair from a nearby stack and wedged it under the knob. Hamstersaurus Rex gave a growl and pawed at the carpet.

"DESTWOY," said a Snuzzle, muffled through the door.

THUMP! It slammed into the door again, harder this time.

"So . . . is this, like, a normal part of Model Interplanetary Council?" said Drew.

"Afraid not," I said.

"When you activated that broken Snuzzle it

must have wirelessly spread the Saw's computer virus to any other Snuzzles within range," said Martha. "And I'm guessing they, in turn, spread it to all the others at the competition."

"But with all the kids here, there must be a hundred Snuzzles," said Dylan. "Are you saying that every one of them is evil now?"

Martha nodded.

"And if I'm understanding correctly, that's *not* a good thing?" said Drew.

"No, it is not!" yelled Martha. "Drew, I have tried to be patient with you but you have to be the single densest person I have ever had the—"

"Lay off him, Martha," I said. "He didn't know what he was doing."

"Thanks, Sam," said Dylan quietly.

Martha took a deep breath. "You're right," she said. "This is all my fault. I should have warned you, Drew. Sorry."

"So outside that door it's basically like an adorable zombie Snuzzle nightmare?" said Drew.

"It's a Cutepocalypse," I said.

"And instead of winning Best Delegation," said

Martha, "our challenge now is to make it out of this hotel alive."

CRACK! One of the chair's legs snapped as the door burst open and a red-eyed Snuzzle tumbled into the ballroom. The Snuzzle scrambled to its feet. "DESTWOY!" it said as it charged at Hamstersaurus Rex.

But the little guy was ready. He spun and kicked it hard against the wall, shattering it.

"Guys, I think we need to go," I said.

We ran out into the hallway. To the right, there were six Snuzzles toddling straight for us. To the left, there were three more.

"Which way?" said Dylan.

"Left!" said Martha.

We ran straight at them. With a snarl, Hamstersaurus Rex lowered his head and rammed the Snuzzle in front, knocking it into another and sending them both sprawling. A deft kick from Dylan sent the third one bouncing away, clearing a path for all of us.

"STEAWTH MODE DISENGAGED!" said an unseen fourth Snuzzle as it sprang out from

DESTWOY!
DESTWOY!
DESTWOY!

behind some curtains. "DESTWOY!"

The Snuzzle tackled Hamstersaurus Rex and smashed him against the wall hard enough to dislodge a chunk of plaster. Hammie was stunned. This gave the other three other Snuzzles a chance to dog-pile on top of the little guy.

"Get off him, you battery-operated creeps!" I cried. But before I could help, Hamstersaurus Rex roared and burst out of the pile, sending the four Snuzzles flying. Without his pups to worry about, Hammie was in full-on rampage mode. Even so, I doubted he could handle four Snuzzles at once, and the other six were closing in fast.

"Come on, little guy!" I said. "Leave them and live to fight another day! You'll get them next time!"

Reluctantly, Hamstersaurus Rex broke off his attack and we all started to run. The Snuzzles were relentless, but we were faster. We rounded a corner and found ourselves at the end of a long hallway lined with hotel rooms. It was empty except for one of the gold-painted kids from Excelsion Prime, who looked panicked.

"Excuse me. Has anybody seen my Snuzzle?" she said. "Its name is Fobo and it likes tummy rubs and secrets and—"

"Run!" yelled Dylan as we blew past the girl.

"Huh?" said the gold-painted girl.

"DESTWOY!" The pack of ten Snuzzles rounded the corner behind us, marching in terrifying formation.

The Excelsion Prime girl screamed and followed us.

"This way, then turn right at the ice machine," said Martha as she led us through the labyrinthine bowels of the hotel.

We ran down several seemingly identical halls until we burst through a set of double doors and found ourselves back at Conference Room B—the Chamber of Unity. The massive hurricane-shaped model of the Milky Way spun lazily over the room, which was now empty now save for two coaches: Coach Weekes and the bald, gray alien guy I'd seen earlier.

"What is happening!" screamed the girl from Excelsion Prime.

"Don't be upset," said Drew, who sounded pretty shaky himself. "This isn't a normal part of Model Interplanetary Council."

"Did you kids win yet?" said Coach Weekes, looking up from the sudoku book.

"No, Leslie!" cried Martha. "We have to leave! Now!"

Martha started toward the room's main entrance.

"Aw, you can't just give up when the chips are down, Cherie," said Coach Weekes. "Don't you know there's a mighty wolf spirit that dwells deep within each of—"

"DESWTOY!" A hidden Snuzzle popped up from underneath the Proxima Centauri b team's placard and flung itself at Hamstersaurus Rex. Without missing a beat, the little guy dodged and chomped down on the Snuzzle's head. With a powerful crunch, plastic shards and wires went flying.

"Fobo!" wailed the Excelsion Prime girl, picking up a handful of Snuzzle bits. "Nooooooooo!"

"Look," said Dylan. "We're too late."

The doors of the main entrance swung open to reveal a dozen red-eyed Snuzzles standing behind them.

"Every coach for himself!" screamed Coach Weekes as he dove underneath a nearby table.

Two of the Snuzzles slammed the main entrance doors shut and a third slid a brass stanchion through the handles.

"They just barred the doors," said Dylan. "I didn't know they could do that."

"On their own, these toys are capable of learning simple tricks and phrases," said Martha. "It's only a guess, but perhaps as more Snuzzles get added to the hive mind, their intelligence increases."

"Well, that's not terrifying at all," said Dylan.

"Personally I find it quite terrifying," said Martha.

"This is not the time to finally explain sarcasm to you, Martha!" said Dylan.

"'Sup!" said Drew, tugging at my sleeve and pointing frantically in another direction. "'Sup! 'Sup! 'Sup!"

More Snuzzles were pouring through the other exit on the opposite side of Conference Room B. They quickly slammed and barred that door as well.

"We're blocked," said Martha. "We'll have to go back the way we came." She turned toward the girl from Excelsion Prime and held out her hand. "Come with us if you want to live."

"I can't go on without Fobo," blubbered the girl.

"Suit yourself!" said Dylan. She turned to the exit, then froze.

"DESTWOY!" called a Snuzzle not far behind us. The pack that had been trailing us finally caught up.

An ominous sound now echoed throughout Conference Room B. Dozens of adorable voices chanting in unison: "DESTWOY! . . . DESTWOY! . . . DESTWOY!"

Dylan, Drew, Martha, Hammie, and I backed into the center of the room.

The Snuzzles converged on us from all sides, forming a ring. Martha jabbed at one with her Scepter of Authority. Dylan swatted another with the heavy spiral-bound Zoblorg VII info packet. Hamstersaurus Rex smashed one with his tail. But it was no use. They kept coming.

"Guys, they're after Hamstersaurus Rex! We're just secondary targets!" I said. "Try to protect the little guy!"

Dylan leaped between Hammie and a group of approaching Snuzzles. One of them hurled a placard at her and she just managed to duck. "Sam, there's too many of them!" yelled Dylan. "They're going to overrun us."

"Hamstersaurus Rex needs to retreat but there's nowhere for him to go," said Martha, kicking over a table to block the onslaught of Snuzzles from her direction. "They've barred all the exits. We're totally surrounded."

My mind raced as I frantically glanced around the room for any way to escape. Every route had been cut off by the Snuzzle hordes. Every route . . . except one. A plan suddenly formed in my mind.

"I have an idea," I cried. "Hold them off, Martha!"

Martha leaped forward, brandishing her Scepter of Authority.

"Drew, Dylan, I need your matching scarves!" I cried.

The two of them froze. Then Dylan gave Drew a small nod.

"Okay, Sam," said Drew. "I don't give up a scarf lightly, so I hope this is important."

"Trust me," I said. "It is."

Dylan and Drew pulled off their scarves—made of stretchy rubber inner tubes—and I quickly knotted their ends together. Meanwhile, Martha swung her Scepter of Authority wildly, barely keeping the advancing Snuzzles at bay.

"Now each of you hold on," I said.

Drew and Dylan each grabbed an end and stretched the rubbery scarf-band tight.

Martha swung her scepter at a Snuzzle and the broomstick shaft snapped in two. "Sam, whatever you're doing, you need to hurry up!" she cried, swinging the broken pieces around.

"All right, hop in, Hammie. You know what the plan is," I said. "You're going on a little trip."

Hamstersaurus Rex climbed into the makeshift inner tube slingshot. I extended my index finger to give him the world's tiniest high five.

"Where's he going?" said Drew.

"To the stars," I said. "Ready for launch!"

I pulled the makeshift oversized slingshot back. "Three . . . two . . . one . . . blastoff!"

I launched Hamstersaurus Rex straight up. The little guy gave a startled yip as he went somersaulting through the air. Just past the apex of his flight, he landed gently on top of the Perseus Arm of the Milky Way model that hung above the room. The mobile slowly spun and swayed as Hamstersaurus Rex peeped over the edge.

"Ha!" cried Dylan, clambering over a table to get away from the Snuzzles that were swarming toward us. "Let's see you adorable one-foot-tall creeps try and get him up there."

The rest of us ran, too. We regrouped on the dais behind the Galactic Consul General's podium, where we found the gold Excelsion Prime girl crying and cradling the remains of her poor departed Fobo.

But the Snuzzles didn't follow us. They had all frozen. Hamstersaurus Rex was now thirty feet above them and they had no obvious way up. One of the Snuzzles jumped straight up—three feet was a surprisingly high vertical, but still nowhere near high enough. Hamstersaurus Rex made a little chittering noise that sounded like laughter.

"So he's safe now?" said Drew.

"I don't think so," said Martha under her breath.

"Look at that."

"TAWGET OUT OF WANGE," said one of the Snuzzles. "INITIATE PYWAMID SEQUENCE."

Immediately several of them got down on all fours in a neat row. Another group climbed on top of them and another group climbed on top of those. The Snuzzles were literally stacking themselves up toward the Milky Way mobile.

"They're making themselves into a living tower!" said Martha. "Like tropical ants."

Dylan hurled her Zoblorg VII info packet at the

pyramid, knocking six Snuzzles off the top, but a second later another six had taken their place. The swaying pyramid was growing taller by the second. In a matter of moments, they would get to Hamstersaurus Rex.

"All right, little guy," I yelled. "You know what to do!"

Hamstersaurus Rex ran down the spiral arm toward the center of the galaxy and disappeared from view. Meanwhile, the rising stack of Snuzzles had nearly made it to the mobile. The top Snuzzle strained to reach. One of its little three-fingered paws got a grip and it started to hoist itself up.

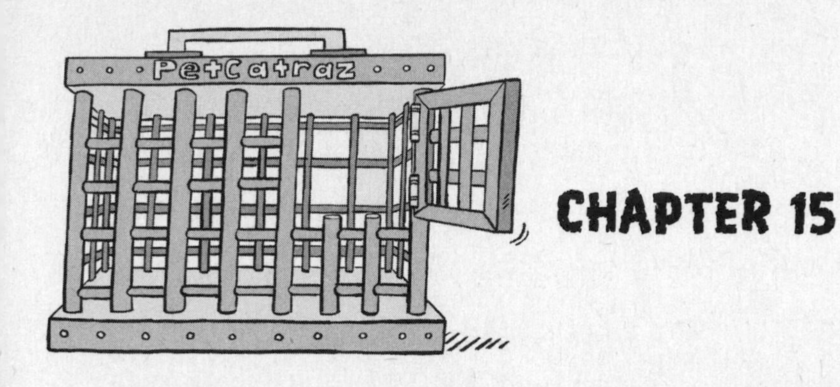

CHAPTER 15

THE TOP SNUZZLE pulled itself up onto the outer arm of the model galaxy. It was followed by another and another. They were clambering aboard by the dozen now.

"DESTWOY," said the Snuzzles as they crept toward the center of the swaying mobile.

"What are we supposed to do?" said Dylan. "They've got him!"

"Not quite," I said.

Suddenly, there was a loud pop and the entire galaxy shifted. Then it fell. For a split second before it hit the ground, there was silence, then, a horrendous crash. Flying placards, desk chairs,

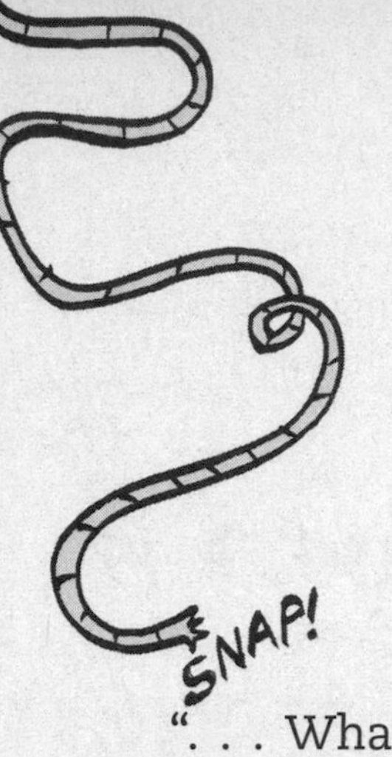

and model star clusters filled the air. I ducked behind the podium to avoid getting pelted with flying Milky Way debris.

After that the Chamber of Unity was quiet.

". . . What happened?" wailed Coach Weekes from underneath his table on the other side of the room. "Is this another giant squirrel attack?"

"Hamstersaurus Rex dropped a galaxy on the Snuzzles," I said.

Sure enough, above us the heavy cable that had suspended the mobile had been gnawed clean through!

But where was Hammie Rex? The mobile's fall had knocked up a thick cloud of dust that filled the room and it was impossible to see more than a few feet ahead. I made my way toward the pile of rubble at the middle of the chamber. As I got closer, I saw that the Snuzzle pyramid had been pulverized. The toys lay in pieces and twisted piles; some of them were still moving weakly but most were crushed beyond all recognition. If they weren't remorseless robotic killing machines I almost would have felt sorry for them. I mean, they *were* pretty cute.

"Sam!" called Martha from somewhere behind me. "Do you see Hamstersaurus Rex anywhere?"

"No," I said. "He must have fallen, too."

I blinked the dust out of my eyes as I searched the wreckage for the little guy. The air cleared for a moment and I spotted him—lying twenty feet away on a pile of crushed Snuzzles and shattered placards.

"Hammie, are you okay?" I called.

The little guy shifted. Whew! The fall must have knocked him unconscious, but at least he was still alive. Before I could reach him, though, a tall figure waded out of the billowing dust. It was the bald gray-alien coach, and he was carrying a PETCATRAZ Pro™, and I suddenly knew where I'd seen the guy before—though I must admit this was by far his best disguise yet.

"Gordon Renfro!" I cried.

Without hesitating, Renfro knelt and quickly scooped up Hamstersaurus Rex. Then he dropped the little guy into the cage, locked it, and ran—immediately disappearing into the haze of Milky Way dust.

"Sam?" called Dylan from somewhere. "Where are you?"

I ran after Renfro but I couldn't see where he'd gone. Somewhere nearby I heard a door open and shut. He was getting away! I headed in the direction of the sound when something smacked into my legs. I tripped and fell, painfully banging my knee on an overturned table leg.

As it clawed at my jeans, the top half of a Snuzzle wheezed, "DESTW—"

Dylan stomped on it.

"Quick! Renfro's escaping!" I cried.

"That guy!" said Dylan, pounding her fist into her palm.

"To the exit!" I said.

She yanked me to my feet and we ran toward the double doors of the main entrance. But they were still barred from the inside.

"Ugh, no," I yelled. "He must have gone out one of the other doors!"

There was a pounding on the main doors. "Hello?" called someone from the other side. "What's going on in there?"

"Let us in!" yelled someone else.

Dylan pulled the stanchion out of the handles and a crowd of shocked MIC delegates flooded into Conference Room B. They were confused and terrified at the scene of destruction inside.

"What happened in here?" said Galactic Consul General Fatima Jabour. "No fighting in the Chamber of Unity!"

“Has anyone seen my Snuzzle?” said one of the L. L. Dupree kids.

“This entire room has been trashed!” cried an MIC judge. “We’re never going to get our security deposit back now.”

“DESTWOY!” said one of the broken Snuzzles, startling several nearby kids.

That Snuzzle lurched toward another one and the two of them grabbed on to each other. A third Snuzzle—this one missing its head—crawled out from under a chair and clung to those two. The hotel lights flickered again.

“Quick, we need to check the other two exits,” I said to Dylan.

“I’ll go left, you go right,” she said.

We split up and each ran for one of the other doors. Dylan’s must have still been barred, because the door we had entered wasn’t. Sure enough, a pair of dusty footprints led away down the SnoozeKing Suites’ carpeted hallway.

“Renfro went this way!” I called back to the others.

But there was no time to wait. I ran after him.

The footprints soon faded and I found myself lost. I had to double back a few times but eventually I spotted a side exit leading to the parking lot. I stumbled out of the dim corridor into the bright sunlight just in time to see a blue sedan peel out of the far end of the parking lot.

"Too late!" I yelled.

"Too late for what?" said Serena.

I turned to see that she and Beefer Vanderkoff had just pulled up on their bikes.

"Dude, you're covered in dirt," said Beefer. "Take a shower once in a while, Sam. This is exactly why you got the nickname The Incredible Stinking Stinkbag."

"I'm dusty because a giant model of the Milky Way—ah, never mind, there's no time to explain!" I said. "The car that just sped away belonged to Gordon Renfro!"

"That guy?!" said Serena and Beefer.

"Yep. And he's got Hamstersaurus Rex," I said. "Quick, I need to borrow one of your bikes."

"Sam, you're never going to catch him on a twenty-one-speed," said Serena.

The car had already disappeared around a bend in the road. She was right.

"Ugh," I said, slumping down on the curb. "I should have known Gordon Renfro would turn back up at the worst possible moment."

"Yeah, that's his signature move," said Serena. "The good news is that there might be someone who can tell you where he's taken Hammie."

"Who?" I said.

"So after I filmed him buying up all that Dino-blast Powerpacker, I decided to look a little more into Rupert MacFarquhar. I wasn't having much luck poking around online, but that's because I was misspelling 'MacFarquhar.'"

"Understandable," I said.

"It really isn't spelled like it sounds. Another strike against the guy," said Serena. "Anyway, after searching a bit more with the correct spelling, I learned that there is a scientist by that name from the UK. And guess who his most recent employer was?"

"SmilesCorp," I said.

"Bingo. He worked there up until the

bankruptcy," said Serena. "Let me show you." She pulled out her smartphone and paused. She looked confused and banged on the side of it. "Stupid phone . . . I'm on my dad's unlimited data plan. I don't understand what's wrong."

She held it up. Odd numbers and characters were flashing around all over the screen. It was just like what happened to the library computers when we activated the Snuzzle. Before I could say anything, there was a loud boom in the distance, followed by the tinkle of broken glass.

"What was that?" said Serena.

"Werewolves," said Beefer ominously.

"I think it might be something even worse," I said.

We rounded the corner just in time to see a bulky shape smash through a set of glass doors of the SnoozeKing's main lobby.

"Dude . . . what?" said Beefer.

I didn't have an immediate answer. At first glance it looked like a six-foot-tall furball. But as it got closer I could see that it was composed of dozens of Snuzzles—some broken, some whole—all

clinging to one another, and moving in unison to somehow roll forward.

"It's like a giant Snuzzle hive-mind amoeba thing," said Serena. "Of all the times not to be able to capture HD shareable video content!" Her smartphone screen was still flickering odd symbols and characters.

"Shhh. Get down!" I hissed.

The three of us ducked behind a parked car.

"WOCATING PWIMAWY TAWGET," boomed the dozens of saccharine voices of the weird Snuzzle-thing as it rolled through the parking lot, setting off car alarms. "WOCATING PWIMAWY TAWGET . . ."

The Snuzzle-thing continued to roll out onto the road, heading back toward the heart of Maple Bluffs. As it did, a nearby stoplight started rapidly cycling through all its colors.

"Okay, I will admit Model Interplanetary Council is slightly more exciting than I thought," said Beefer.

Terrified MIC delegates and coaches now began to spill out of the broken lobby doors, some screaming, others crying. A few recognized Beefer from Epic Ninja 360-Degree Fail and demanded autographs, which he angrily refused. The parking lot was pandemonium. I saw Martha, Dylan, and Drew cutting their way through the crowd.

"Over here!" I called to them. "I couldn't catch Gordon Renfro. And he's got Hamstersaurus Rex."

"Sorry, Sam," said Dylan.

"That is very, very bad," said Martha. "What might be worse is the malicious wireless signal that Snuzzle-ball is broadcasting seems to be highly disruptive to all electronics. And the more Snuzzles it adds to the collective, the stronger the signal gets."

"So people's phones don't work?" I said. "I mean, that's annoying, but it isn't exactly life-threatening, is it?"

"To me it is!" yelled Serena, who was still frantically trying to fix her smartphone.

"What if somebody needs to call 911?" said Martha. "But it's worse than that. We rely on computers for everything from checking out library books to running our hospitals. Look at what it did to that stoplight."

The stoplight on the corner was still flashing crazily.

"Would that prevent a car accident?" said Martha.

"So we have to stop the Snuzzle-thing ASAP," I said.

"But we also have to save Hamstersaurus Rex," said Dylan. "We swore an oath."

"Then let's split up and meet back at the secret Hamster Monitor emergency rendezvous point at 0400 hours," said Martha. "Dylan, Drew, and I will follow the Snuzzle-thing and try to figure out how to defeat it. Sam, you, Serena, and Beefer focus on rescuing Hamstersaurus Rex."

"I think I know just where to start," I said.

Serena, Beefer, and I found Cid Wilkins in the lobby of the SnoozeKing Suites, amid the thinning crowd. He looked ecstatic.

"Sam Dunk, did you see that thing? It just smashed through the doors like KABLAMMO!" he said, pantomiming. "Man, I *knew* living in Maple

Bluffs would be cooler than Monaco!"

"Cid, I hate to tell you this, but your manny really is evil," I said.

"Say again, laddie?" said Rupert, stepping out from a plastic palm tree.

"Rupert MacFarquhar," I said, "tell me what Gordon Renfro has done with Hamstersaurus Rex!"

Rupert squinted at me and crossed his arms. "I cannae answer your questions on that subject, lad," he said. "I am bound by a standard nondisclosure agreement. You can direct all inquiries to my employer."

"Who?" I said. "SmilesCorp?"

Rupert said nothing.

"No," said Cid. "He means me."

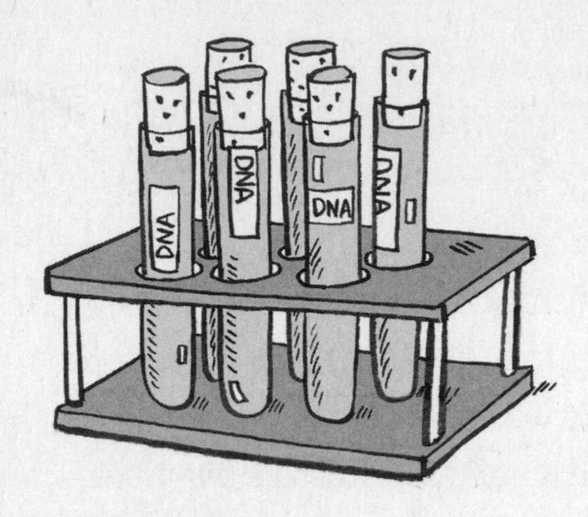

CHAPTER 16

"LET ME EXPLAIN," said Cid. "Before I came to Maple Bluffs, I got really, really into Hamstersaurus Rex. Great article, by the way, Serena."

"Thanks?" said Serena.

"I mean, the little guy is just so awesome," said Cid. "The superstrength, the tail, the mysterious origin story. I totally dig it."

"Yeah, I know all that," I said. "So?"

"So you've been to my house," said Cid. "I've got every toy a kid could ever want, right? I've got a waterslide and a prerelease Gamehouser APEX 900 Black and a bowling alley that I don't even use. I hate bowling! But the one thing I don't have is a pet mutant hamster-dinosaur hybrid. That's why I convinced my dad to bring Rupert on board."

"On board? You specifically hired Rupert to . . . make you your own mutant hamster?" I said.

"More or less," said Cid. "I figured with enough money it should be possible. Why not?"

Serena shuddered. "Creepy much?" she said.

"No, it's not creepy," said Cid, showing a flash of irritation that I'd never seen before. "It's just not fair that Sam gets a Hamstersaurus Rex and I don't. I mean, how is that—"

"Hang on," I said. "You literally moved your entire family to this town so you could figure out how to somehow re-create Hamstersaurus Rex."

"Yeah, well, I thought Rupert might need to do some firsthand research. Maybe collect a few samples of Hamstersaurus Rex DNA or something?" said Cid. "Anyway, moving is no biggie. Neither is buying a house, if I'm being perfectly honest. I'm in sixth grade and I've already gone to nine different schools in four different countries. What's a few months in this weird little town, more or less?"

"No wonder your sister, Sarah, was so upset

about coming here," I said. "It was all for you."

"Sarah-Anne has always been a whiner," said Cid. "That's why she never gets her way. It's so easy once you realize that for my dad, grand gestures are easier than actually, you know, parenting. Anyway, hopefully my sis will learn that you catch more flies with honey."

". . . Like pretending to be someone's friend," I said.

Cid shrugged. "Hey, don't get me wrong, Sam Dunk. You're cool," he said. "But friends are a dime a dozen. Mutant dino-hamsters? Those are rare. Our relationship was a means to an end. Nothing personal." Cid held up his hands like anyone would be crazy to get upset.

"Sam, I'm pretty tempted to use my bullying skills for good here," whispered Beefer. "You want me to flatten this kid?"

"Not yet," I said. "So Rupert obviously failed to clone Hamstersaurus Rex."

Rupert blinked. Cid sputtered something that sounded like the beginning of a justification. I cut him off.

"That is what you needed 'DNA samples' for, isn't it?" I said. "Which were conveniently provided by all the fur and skin cells Hammie shed while we were hanging out at your house."

"Yeah, you're right," said Cid. "The cloning method proved to be more difficult than we'd anticipated."

"I'm guessing Rupert realized he would need PaleoGro for the process, hence all the Dinoblast Powerpacker," I said. "The 'DO NOT ENTER' room was Rupert's lab. But you cleaned it up by the time you showed me what was inside."

"Yep. We just moved it to another empty room down the hall," said Cid. "In retrospect, that ominous sign probably made it way more suspicious. Lessons learned."

I turned to Rupert. "Still, your second scientific effort must have been tanking, too."

"Watch your tone, lad," said Rupert. "I have a PhD in genetics from the University of Paisley Online—"

"You blew it," I said. "Or else you wouldn't have needed Gordon Renfro to abduct Hamstersaurus

Rex so you can keep him for yourself. Would you, Cid?"

Cid looked horrified. "Hang on just a minute," he said. "Gordon Renfro did what? Hamstersaurus Rex isn't in your backpack right now? Homerun, are you in there? I have some Funchos for—"

"Don't play dumb, Cid," I said. "Renfro just sped away with Hammie locked in a PETCATRAZ Pro™, probably to a private jet you chartered to fly him to the Azores or Maldives or some other plural rich-people place halfway around the world!"

"Sam, seriously," said Cid, "I had nothing to do with that! I don't even know Gordon Renfro!"

"Yeah right," I said. "What I still don't understand is why it is you reprogrammed the Snuzzles to 'destroy' the little guy. Was it all just an elaborate distraction? You could have just pulled the fire alarm, dude!"

"I'm not responsible for those Snuzzles either. I wasn't lying about that," said Cid. "You have to understand, I would never ever want to *kill* Hamstersaurus Rex! I want to *own* him!"

I stared at Cid for a long moment.

"Ugh," I said. "As much as it makes my skin crawl to hear you say that, I . . . actually believe you. So help me out, Rupert: If SmilesCorp doesn't exist anymore and Renfro's not working for Cid, then why in the world does he still want Hamstersaurus Rex?"

Rupert silently shifted. He still wasn't going to violate his nondisclosure agreement without employer permission.

"Go on, answer him," said Cid.

Rupert gave a yellow smirk. "Oh, SmilesCorp still exists, laddie," he said. "The corporation merely had one of its own subsidiaries purchase the parent company for a PR facelift. Don't be fooled, though. It might technically be called Pappy's Beeswax of Maine now, but SmilesCorp is going strong."

CHAPTER 17

"...YOU'RE GETTING EYE grease on them," said Beefer.

"Am not!" said Serena. "My eyes are probably the least greasy of any of us."

"Just tell us what you see!" I said.

Serena lowered Beefer's binoculars. "No lights on," she said. "Doesn't look like anybody's home. But that's what they'd want us to think, isn't it?"

We crouched in the bushes at the far edge of a wide, empty parking lot. It was quiet here, and in recent months weeds had started to grow up through cracks in the pavement. By all appearances the SmilesCorp campus was locked and deserted. Still, I was sure this was where we would find Hamstersaurus Rex. And with him: Gordon Renfro.

"We've got to check inside," I said.

"Just like the Michael Perkins rescue mission! Man, I *love* sequels. They're always better than the original," said Beefer. "Okay. Masks on, people."

The three of us pulled on the personalized ninja masks Beefer had thoughtfully sewn for us—Beefer's was covered in music notes; Serena's was purple, which no longer matched her green hair; and mine was made to look like Hamstersaurus Rex. We crept across the parking lot toward Building Seven: the location of SmilesCorp's Genetic Research and Development Lab.

We tried several doors. All locked.

"Here," I said. "Let me use my mom's old ID card." I swiped it through the security scanner

beside the fire exit. The scanner beeped and the light flashed red. "No dice."

"But at least now we know the building still has power," said Serena. "The lights might be off but somebody's definitely inside."

"So how do we get in?" I said. "Without Hammie Rex, busting down the door is a nonstarter."

"Don't be an idiotic moron, Sam. We don't need brute strength here. We need *my* specialty: finesse," said Beefer. "Infiltrating a locked fortress is a fairly advanced ninja technique. But nothing a clear belt like me can't handle." He did a complicated ninja bow that ended with double peace signs.

I sighed. "Come on, man. You remember what happened at the flea market? You really don't have to do this."

Serena's eyes lit up. "Oh yes he does!" she said. "This is what I've been waiting for! Sam, give me your camera. My phone might be fried, but there's no way I'm not filming whatever Beefer does next. He's about to create some more amazing hashtagninjafail viral content for my blog!"

"Beefer," I said, "trust me that this is a sentence

I never thought I would say, but: I don't want you to hurt yourself."

Beefer put a hand on my shoulder. "I know you're faint of heart, Sam, and you're probably feeling super scared right now," he said. "But you don't need to worry, little fellow. It's time for me to redeem myself and restore my ninja honor. Go on. Give her your camera. Today I remembered my grappling hook."

I handed Serena my UltraLite SmartShot. Beefer reached into his duffel bag and pulled a four-pronged metal hook tied to a long rope. He started to swing it around over his head. I ducked. Serena hit record.

"Ninja grappling wall-scale maneuver . . . GO!" yelled Beefer. He let the grappling hook fly. It arced high into the air and landed on top of Building Seven with a clang. Beefer yanked the rope and it held fast, apparently hooked on something. Beefer took a deep breath and then deftly shimmied up the rope and disappeared onto the roof without a sound. Serena and I looked at each other in disbelief.

"He didn't smash into anything or break any bones," said Serena.

"It didn't even look like he got a rope burn," I said. "Maybe he is a—"

"Real ninja?" said Beefer as he threw open the door from the inside. "Of course I am." Beefer turned right to the camera and gave a thumbs-up. "And you can be, too, if you stay in school, kids."

Serena sighed and lowered the UltraLite SmartShot. "Great. None of this footage is usable."

And so the three of us stepped out of the afternoon sun and into the darkened laboratory. It was eerily quiet; very different from the screeching, squawking, and howling of mutant animals that filled the air last time Beefer and I had been here. Much of the scientific equipment was now covered in tarps and drop cloths to keep the dust off.

"Look," said Serena. There were two clear sets of footprints leading away through a layer of dust on the floor. One matched Beefer's sneakers. The other didn't.

"I didn't see anybody on the stairs down from the roof," said Beefer. "And my highly trained senses are much more attuned to my surroundings than yours are. Because, as you both saw, I am a real ninja."

"All right, all right. We get it. The rope-climbing thing was cool," said Serena. "But now we have to find Hamstersaurus Rex."

"Let's follow the tracks," I said.

Beefer, Serena, and I traced the footprints in the dust as they passed rows of empty cages and drained tanks and led us deeper into the dark lab.

"Hey . . . you guys see that?" said Beefer.

There was light coming from a corner. As we got closer, I saw that it was a large, shiny aluminum sphere with a computer console attached. On it was a handwritten label that read "Specimen #4449." The glowing monitor showed several continuous readings of scientific data. The numbers were gibberish to me. The dust tracks looked like they had lingered here on multiple occasions.

"What do you think it is?" I said.

"It looks like a baby werewolf incubator to me," said Beefer.

"Great," I said. "And do you have any theories, Serena?"

Serena studied the monitor. "No idea what most of these numbers mean, but this one kind of looks like a heart rate."

She pointed to a number that bounced around between 350 and 450. There was a little heart icon beside it.

"A heart rate that fast would probably have to be something tiny," said Serena.

"Like a mutant hamster," I said.

I found a latch on the aluminum sphere and unfastened it. The whole strange device opened up like a giant clamshell. Inside was a rodent. All four of its legs were restrained with heavy straps, and patches of its fur had been shaved where various wires, sensors, electrodes, and an IV drip had been attached. But the creature wasn't Hamstersaurus Rex.

"The Mind Mole!" said Serena.

The three of us recoiled in horror. But the Mind Mole

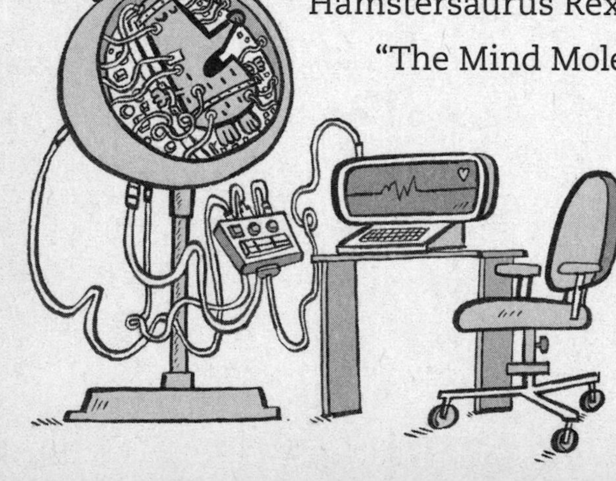

didn't move. He was unconscious. And whatever Gordon Renfro was dosing him with was strong enough to keep him that way. We looked at each other, afraid and unsure of what to do.

"What are you waiting for?" said Beefer. "That's *worse* than a baby werewolf! Slam that metal ball shut right now and never, ever open it again."

I hesitated.

"I—I don't know," I said.

"Sam, he literally mind-controlled you," said Serena. "He tried to drop a five-hundred-pound tiki god on your head. I could go on."

"Yeah, I know he's rotten. Maybe evil," I said. "But even he doesn't deserve . . . *this*. I mean, look at him."

The Mind Mole was small and pitiful under the sickly glare of the computer monitor. His beady eyes twitched underneath his lids.

"It was getting scientifically tortured by Gordon Renfro that warped his giant brain in the first place," I said.

"So . . . what exactly do you propose?" said Serena.

"Follow me," I said. "I think I have an idea."

We found the lab's kitchenette. Sure enough, there was still a roll of aluminum foil in a drawer in the pantry. We each wrapped enough of the stuff around our heads to make Old Man Ohlman proud. Then we cautiously returned to the Mind Mole's globe-prison.

"You sure about this?" said Serena.

"I am," I said.

I took a deep breath, and then I started to pull the wires and sensors off. At last, I carefully removed the Mind Mole's IV sedative drip. The three of us ducked back behind a covered lab cart and waited.

With a startled squeal, the Mind Mole sat upright. He blinked, and then his eyes darted around the dark lab, gleaming with malice. He looked furious. I got a familiar static-electricity feeling as the hairs of my arms started to stand up. With a flick of his paw, the lab cart we were hiding behind telekinetically shot across the room and slammed into the wall.

I swallowed. ". . . Go on," I said. "Shoo! Get out of here! Make your grand escape or whatever!"

The Mind Mole didn't budge.

"You're free!" I said. "You don't need to hurt anyone today. Just go, okay?"

"Sam, look!" whispered Serena.

All around us flasks, clipboards, Bunsen burners, and other loose pieces of lab equipment started to shake and then to slowly float upward. The Mind Mole glared at me with his horrible eyes. I couldn't tell if he was trying to hypnotize me but I had to wonder if I had just made a colossal mistake. Our tinfoil hats wouldn't protect us much if he dropped a centrifuge or an industrial freezer or maybe the whole building on our heads.

Instead, the Mind Mole let the floating objects clatter to the floor. With another loud squeal he scurried in the direction of the exit.

". . . Wow. I don't ever get scared of anything ever," said Beefer, clutching his chest. "But if I did, that would have been the perfect time."

"Boo," said Serena.

Beefer leaped two feet into the air. "Don't *do* that!"

"Guys, look," I said.

The dusty tracks led away down a corridor. We followed them until at last we came to a familiar office. It was the room with the wall displaying the portraits of all the SmilesCorp lab chiefs, past and present. Among them was Gordon Renfro's face, bald and menacing. I shuddered. But I wasn't looking for him.

"This is the one," I said.

I pointed to the portrait of Sue Sandoval, smiling slightly with a kindly twinkle in her eye.

"My great-aunt Sue," said Serena. "Man, I miss her so much."

Serena touched the painting. As she did, the frame spun ninety degrees clockwise. There was a click and then a low rumbling noise. The entire portrait wall slowly slid aside to reveal a heavy metal door. Beside the door was an electronic keypad.

"This is where Hamstersaurus Rex is being held," I said. "I'm sure of it."

"Oh yeah," said Serena. "Aunt Sue's notes mentioned something like this—a top secret SmilesCorp lab that had a top top secret lab hidden inside it, where she used to work. Hang on. I'm pretty sure I know the combination."

Serena punched in a six-digit code. The light flashed green and the door's mechanical lock unbolted.

"What was it?" I said.

Serena grinned. "My birthday."

We pushed the heavy door open, revealing stairs that led down.

CHAPTER 18

THE THREE OF us quietly crept down several long flights of stairs to a subbasement that must have been pretty far belowground. We followed a hallway to a windowed set of double doors. Cautiously I peeked through one of the windows.

The room beyond was a large, brightly lit laboratory. It was filled with high-tech equipment, much of which looked like futuristic weaponry in various stages of development. There were various shelves lined with canisters labeled "PaleoGro" and "Huginex-G" and many other SmilesCorp chemicals I didn't recognize. At the far side of the room was a bald man in a lab coat with his back to us, typing at a computer: Gordon Renfro!

Beefer tapped me on the shoulder and pointed. Not far from Renfro was a clear plastic enclosure containing an odd device that almost looked like a piece of miniaturized gym equipment. Strapped into the device was Hamstersaurus Rex.

As quietly as I could, I eased the door open. Serena pulled out the UltraLite SmartShot and started to record.

". . . Nine hundred fifty pounds," said Renfro, logging it on his computer.

Hamstersaurus Rex flexed his legs and the weight-lifting contraption moved. Behind the little guy, a stack of weights rose up a track.

"Impressive," said Renfro. "Increasing the load to a thousand pounds."

He was testing the limits of Hammie's dinosaur superstrength.

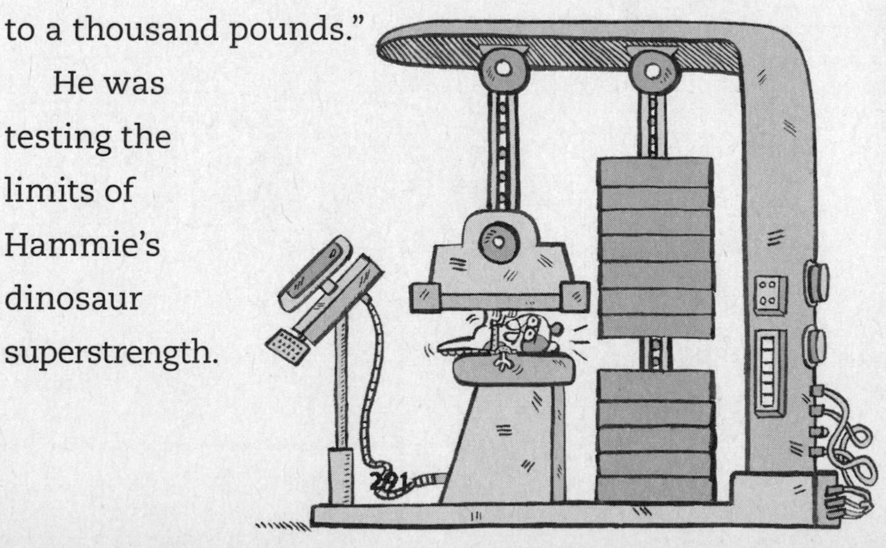

Renfro typed something on his computer. A mechanical arm added another weight to the device with a clank. Hamstersaurus Rex strained with effort.

I had to save the little guy before he got hurt! I started to run to Hammie but I didn't get more than half a step before Gordon Renfro hit a red button mounted on his desk.

SHWOOP! A metal security gate slid shut in front of me, blocking the doorway and completely cutting us off from the laboratory. Red lights began to flash and a computerized voice spoke over the intercom: "Warning. Security breach in Subbasement Laboratory. . . . Warning. Security breach in Subbasement Laboratory. . . ."

"Let us in!" I cried as I pounded on the gate.

Beefer slammed his shoulder against it. It was no use. The gate was made of interlocking steel bars. I doubted even Hamstersaurus Rex could have broken through it.

Gordon Renfro slowly swiveled in his chair and grinned at us. "Well, if it isn't Sam Gibbs, the middle-school intellectual property thief."

"You're the thief!" I yelled. "Give me my hamster back and then stop the Snuzzle virus from hurting anyone else!"

Renfro laughed. "I'm afraid you're mistaken on both counts. First, I had nothing to do with the Snuzzles, that was just a happy coincidence. And second, you cannot steal what you already own. The patent on Specimen Number 00001 belongs to SmilesCo—" Gordon Renfro corrected himself. "Pardon me, *Pappy's Beeswax of Maine.*"

"Keep on blabbing, tough guy," said Serena as she filmed. "This is how we got you last time."

"Ah, and here we have Serena Sandoval, former intern turned investigative journalist," said Renfro. "You know, I think I may like you even less than your great-aunt."

"The feeling is mutual," said Serena.

"Fortunately this time your footage will be confiscated and erased before it can be made public." Gordon Renfro squinted at Beefer. "Ah, and I see now your little band is a trio. . . . Hang on, is that the kid from Epic Ninja 360-Degree Fail?"

"Aw man," said Beefer. "You saw that?"

"Of course," said Gordon Renfro. "Almost as hilarious as the three of you thinking you could sneak in here past all our security cameras. In any event, I have alerted the Pappy's Beeswax of Maine elite security team, who will be arriving any moment. I'd say you have, oh, a minute and a half or so. I hope you don't mind if I return to my work while we wait. . . ." He turned back toward his computer. "Now, shall we try eleven hundred pounds?" The mechanical arm added another weight to the device. Hamstersaurus Rex squealed.

"Why?" I said. "Why do you even want Hammie? What's so important about him?"

"My, my, that is the question, isn't it?" said Renfro. "Specimen Number 00001 represents a true revolution in home security. The product is formidable yet compact enough to fit in your pocket. Imagine a Hamstersaurus Rex in every household! What burglar would want to face him? What mugger?"

"That's it?" I said. "So he's just supposed to be a glorified guard dog?"

"Not quite," said Gordon Renfro. "In truth, we were working on something far more ambitious: we had secured a top secret military contract. But my predecessor, Dr. Sandoval, was shortsighted. She developed ethical qualms about what we were doing here. In the end, she tried to sabotage our work by sneaking 00001 out of this lab, depriving us of him at a critical juncture in our research."

"Why couldn't you just repeat the experiment that created him?" I said.

Gordon Renfro sputtered. "Because we were—we were focused on different—we didn't have the precise—"

"I get it," I said. "It's the same reason your colleague Rupert MacFarquhar couldn't do it."

"You're just not as good a scientist as my

great-aunt Sue," said Serena.

"How dare you!" said Renfro. "I'm better because I'm rational. I don't let my emotions get in the way!" He turned back to his console. "Fifteen hundred pounds!"

The mechanical arm added five more of the large weights to Hamstersaurus Rex's strength-tester. The little guy groaned in anguish. His legs were trembling. He couldn't take it for that much longer.

"Stop!" I cried. "You're hurting him!"

He ignored me. "Most importantly, I have the resolve to take us to the final stages of our project," said Gordon Renfro. "You see, Specimen Number 00001 isn't just a hamster-dinosaur. He's a hamster *and* a dinosaur. You almost stumbled onto the right track when you gave him a dose of Huginex-G to fight Squirrel Kong. That, combined with an ultraconcentrated dose of PaleoGro"—he held up a vial of each—"and this little fellow will truly be combat ready! I cannot *wait* to witness him finally deployed on the field of battle—"

"You like fights, huh? Well, that's good, because

you're about to get one!" I cried. "Sic 'im, kids!"

I reached into my backpack and pulled out three more mutant hamster-dinosaur hybrids: Stompy, Chompy, and Hatshepsut. Maybe *I* couldn't get through the security door, but they sure could! The three tiny pups easily squeezed between the bars and scattered into the laboratory. Their dad was in trouble and they were fighting mad.

"Ah, you've conveniently delivered me three more live specimens," said Gordon Renfro. "Thank you, Sam, that's very . . ."

He trailed off as Hatshepsut leaped onto a shelf full of expensive-looking microscopes.

"No . . . Don't touch those. Bad hamster," said Gordon Renfro, rising. "Bad hamster! Each of those phase-contrast fluorescence microscopes is worth over ten thousand—"

Hatshepsut grinned and shoved one off the edge. Gordon Renfro had to make a flying dive to catch the falling microscope. And he did catch it. But unfortunately for him, this left his haunches wide open for a monster chomp by (you guessed it) Chompy.

"AAAAAAH-ha-ha-hawabagogga!" shrieked Gordon Renfro as Chompy's tiny, needlelike fangs sank in.

CRASH! Another microscope hit the floor nearby, spraying parts and broken glass everywhere. Hatshepsut cackled.

"Get off me! Don't touch any more of those!" cried Gordon Renfro as he frantically tried to dislodge Chompy from his backside while squirming to position himself under the next microscope.

That level of multitasking may explain why he never saw Stompy coming. The hamster pup landed on top of his head, dino-feet first, slamming it into the linoleum floor with a thud.

"Oooooooh," moaned Gordon Renfro. "Did I win Science Night?"

At this point Chompy did dislodge his bite. He scrambled out of the way just before the entire shelf of phase-contrast fluorescence microscopes—which Hatshepsut had somehow managed to tip over—landed right on top of Gordon Renfro.

Hatshepsut guffawed as Chompy started to

chomp his way through a bundle of fiber-optic cables. Meanwhile, Stompy kept on stomping on things. She stomped on a rack of test tubes. She stomped on an external hard drive. She stomped on a small potted plant.

"Stompy, the button!" I cried. "I need you to hit that red button!"

At last she did, landing squarely on the panic button mounted to Gordon Renfro's desk. SWHOOP! The security door slid open. Beefer, Serena, and I rushed into the lab. Using Renfro's computer, we removed all the weights from the strength-tester and extricated Hamstersaurus Rex from the device.

"Good to have you back, little guy," I said as I hugged him close.

Behind me, Gordon Renfro moaned and started to pull himself out from under the wreckage of the microscope shelf. Hammie roared with unbridled fury. If Gordon Renfro was awake, he wanted a piece of the guy.

"No time, Hammie," I said. "Security will be here any second!"

I scooped up the pups, who had taken it upon themselves to destroy several more pieces of expensive-looking lab equipment in the meantime.

"You kids did great, by the way," I said. "I think you might even be better rampagers than your dad!"

Hammie gave them each a proud nuzzle. I tucked the whole hamster family back into my backpack.

"Ninja escape maneuver GO!" cried Beefer as he tossed a smoke bomb onto the floor.

We ran for it.

On our way up the stairs, Serena was already reviewing the footage on my camera. "Another Gordon Renfro confession plus excellent video of him getting his butt kicked by three adorable baby mutant hamsters," she said. "I think I may just have just captured the most shareable web content of all time!"

"Wait," said Beefer. "You don't think it's going to get more hits than Epic Ninja 360-Degree Fail, do you?"

"Yeah, probably!" said Serena.

"Aw, come on!" said Beefer. "That's no fair!"

We reached the top of the stairs and ran

through the hidden portrait door.

"Stop!" called Renfro's voice from the stairwell behind us. "Don't let those children get away."

We rounded a corner and skidded to a halt. The hallway ahead was completely blocked by five security guards who looked more like a SWAT team.

"Freeze!" bellowed the guard in front. "You three are trespassing on private property!"

Hamstersaurus Rex snarled from inside my backpack.

"Hi. I think there's been a big misunderstanding," said Serena. "See, I used to be an intern here so I can totally vouch for these two—"

"Don't move!" yelled the lead guard. "Put your hands up."

We were trapped. We may have been able to take a single arrogant scientist by surprise, but not five guards in riot gear.

"Sam, what do we do?" said Beefer. "I don't know if I can ninja this many guys."

I sighed and put my hands up. "It's over," I said. "They got us."

Gordon Renfro came up behind us, huffing

and puffing. He doubled over to catch his breath.

"I admire your resolve, Sam Gibbs. But you must understand you can't be allowed to escape," said Renfro. "SmilesCorp, ahem, I mean Pappy's Beeswax of Maine, will always come after Specimen Number 00001. We will never rest until our project is rea—"

WHANG! From out of nowhere a flying table pinned Gordon Renfro to the wall.

". . . What just happened?" said the lead security guard.

Before anyone could answer, the five guards were scattered like bowling pins hit by an invisible ball. Standing behind them was a tiny rodent with an oversized head.

". . . The Mind Mole," I whispered.

One of the security guards rose and spoke to me in a grating high-pitched voice. "Yes. Of course it is the Mind Mole. Did you think we would scurry away before we had our exquisite revenge?" The security guard gave a horrible, squealing laugh.

"But we set you free," I said. "We didn't have to do that."

The Mind Mole squinted at me. "Not revenge against you insignificant worms," he said through the mouth of his security guard puppet. "Revenge against the creator; the tormentor. Revenge against Gordon Renfro."

"Now—now, hang on just a minute," said Renfro. "Let's not be hasty! Specimen Number 4449, I fully intended to release you back into the wild once I ran a battery of routine tests—"

"Balderdash!" screeched the hypnotized guard.

Gordon Renfro flinched, still pinned behind the table.

"Sam, you told us earlier that we need not hurt anybody. On this point, we disagree," said the Mind Mole. "Now leave this place. And know that it is we, the Mind Mole, who have graciously freed you. This makes us even."

So Serena, Beefer, and I ran. Hamstersaurus Rex and his three pups were safe. I didn't look back to see what the Mind Mole was about to do to Gordon Renfro but I started to feel the hairs on my arms stand on end. . . .

CHAPTER 19

"SORRY," SAID PATRICIA, the ticket-taker at the Maple Bluffs Antique Doll Museum, "can't let you in."

"But this is the secret Hamster Monitor emergency rendezvous point!" I said.

"No idea what that means," said Patricia. "All I know is that I'm on my lunch break." She held up an egg salad wrap and pointed to a small handwritten note that was stuck to the window. It said "Out to Lunch."

". . . But you're *not* out to lunch," said Serena.

"You don't know that," said Patricia. She drew the blinds.

Norton, the museum security guard, rapped on the glass with his flashlight. “Oh, for crying out loud, just let them in, Patricia,” he said, “or I’ll write you up for stealing all those thumbtacks.”

Patricia pulled the blinds and squinted at Norton. Norton crossed his arms.

“Oh yeah,” he said. “I know *all* about that.”

“Welcome to the Maple Bluffs Antique Doll Museum,” said Patricia as she waved us through the door.

We found the only other patrons—Martha, Dylan, and Drew—poring over a map on a bench near an exhibit called “TransylFUNia: The Childhood Dolls of Vlad the Impaler.”

"'Sup!" said Drew as we approached.

"We got him!" I said. I held Hammie Rex up and the little guy let out a celebratory growl. His three pups joined in. Dylan gave each of them a Mint-Caramel Choconob and Martha was so happy she barely shushed us. I gave the others a quick rundown of our SmilesCorp mission and the rampaging heroism of Stompy, Chompy, and Hatshepsut.

"So what about the giant Snuzzle-monster thing?" said Serena as she played with Stompy. "Have you guys wrapped up that whole deal yet?"

Dylan and Martha looked at each other.

"Well, there's some fantastic news and some, uh, significantly less fantastic news," said Martha. She indicated the map. "You see, about half a mile from the SnoozeKing Suites, the Snuzzle-creature left the main road and cut east through the woods toward Mount Sherman. The fantastic news is that there aren't very many people out there, so it's not going to cause much damage."

The area on the map did look pretty empty, only a few houses here or there.

"What's the less fantastic news?" I said.

"If we're guessing right, this is where it's headed," said Dylan.

Her finger traced a straight line east over the mountain and across the woods, through Cannon Park, and right into the middle of downtown.

"The heart of Maple Bluffs," I said. "But why?"

"The Snuzzle hive mind's goal is still to destroy Hamstersaurus Rex, but at this point it doesn't know where he is," said Martha. "So it's doing the most logical thing: searching all the places it knows he might be."

"Meaning places where Hammie has already had a run-in with an evil Snuzzle," said Dylan. "Assuming it chooses the most direct route, we think that means it will head to Horace Hotwater, then to the library . . . ," said Dylan, connecting the dots on the map in a relatively straight line. She slid her finger to the final location.

". . . And then my house," I said.

Dylan nodded gravely.

"Any ideas on how to stop it before it gets there?" I said.

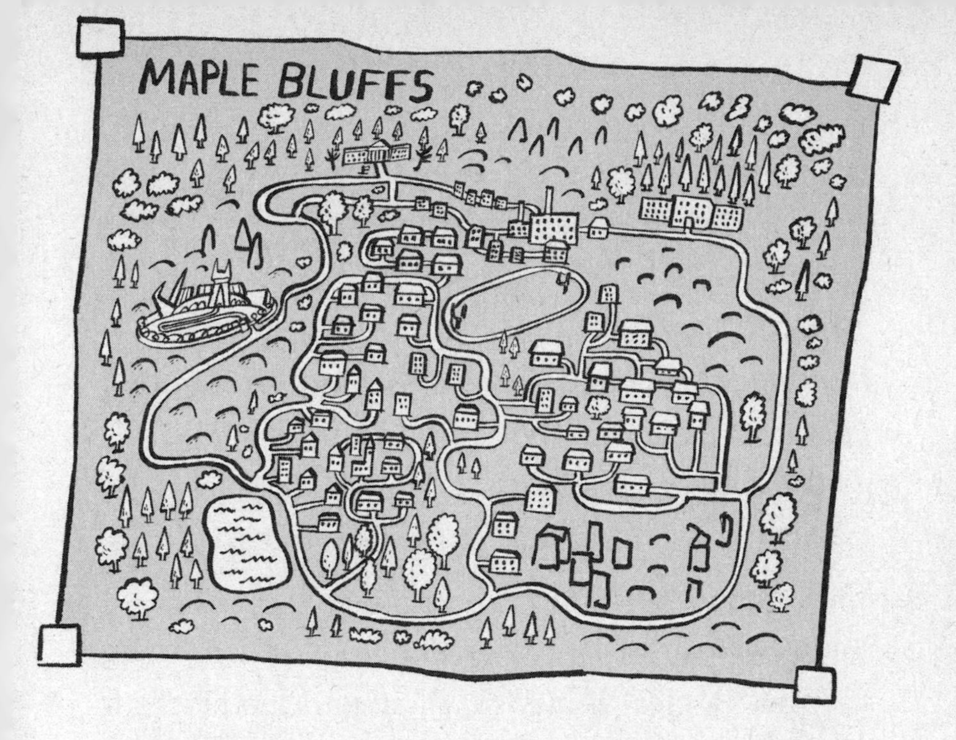

"My idea of hitting it with a gigantic golf disc was deemed impractical," said Drew.

"I still think it was a good plan," said Dylan, patting his hand.

"And I assume you already notified the police," I said.

"They laughed at us," said Dylan. "A lot."

"As a side note, if that's what it feels like to tell a joke, I can't see myself ever doing it," said Martha.

"So what do we do?" I said.

"Well, we know the Snuzzles communicate

wirelessly," said Martha. "That's how the Saw's virus spreads. The simplest way to stop them would be to program a second 'good' virus that overwrites the first one."

"Great!" I said. "Let's do that then. Nice work, team."

"It's not that simple, Sam," said Martha. "It would probably take me weeks to code something as complex as that. Maybe longer because I'm certain the Saw put in various fail-safes and security measures to counteract such a strategy."

"Serena," I said, "you're good with computers—"

"Content, not code, my friend," said Serena. "Sorry."

"Beefer?" I said.

"I feel like I already did my thing, which was the ninja climbing / smoke bomb stuff. Remember?" said Beefer.

"Drew, please tell me you're a secret programming genius," I said.

"No, but I am pretty good at making homemade candles," said Drew. "Could that help?"

"Honestly, Sam," said Martha, "I'm worried

there's only one person who could create a second virus in time: the Saw."

"Perfect," I said. "So we just have to A) figure out who that is and B) convince them to do the complete opposite of their original evil plan."

It didn't look good.

"Guys, there's no reason we can't figure out the Saw's identity," said Serena. "When you're trying to get to the bottom of a mystery, sometimes it's good to start with who you know it isn't and then see who's left."

"It's not Cid Wilkins or Rupert MacFarquhar or Gordon Renfro," I said. "For various reasons, they each wanted Hamstersaurus Rex alive."

"It's not the Mind Mole, because he was unconscious until we set him free," said Serena.

"You set the Mind Mole free?!" said Martha.

"Er, yeah, it was a whole thing," I said, "but there's no time to worry about that now."

"So who else despises Hamstersaurus Rex enough that they would destroy a whole town just to get him?" said Dylan.

None of us had an answer.

"Man, I'm going to miss Maple Bluffs," said Beefer. "It's where I keep most of my stuff."

Suddenly, it hit me. "Wait a second," I said. "That's it."

"What's it?" said Martha.

"It isn't that the Saw hates Hamstersaurus Rex so much that they don't care about Maple Bluffs," I said. "It's that they hate Maple Bluffs! I think I know who it is. . . ."

"Sam Dunk! How's it going, man?" said Cid as he opened the front door. "Wow, truth be told, I thought I'd never see you again. But I'm glad you're not still mad about . . . you know. Oh, and I see you brought Homerun and the kids! Hey, little—"

Hammie and his pups gave a simultaneous snarl and Cid jumped back.

"Out of the way, Cid," I said as I stepped past him into the mansion's foyer. Beefer, Serena, Martha, Dylan, and Drew all followed me inside.

"Looks like we've got a party on our hands," said Cid. "Can I interest any of you in a soda? You can pick any flavor in the world you want."

"Mmm," said Dylan. "How about a soda that tastes like fake friendship?"

Cid blinked. "Not sure we have that," he said. "Can I ask why you're here?"

"I'm looking for Sarah," I said.

"Sarah-Anne?" said Cid. "What do you want with her? She's not impo—"

"Shut *up*, Cid," said Sarah as she descended the spiral staircase clutching her beat-up old laptop.

"Ouch," said Dylan.

"Can I help you with something or whatever?" said Sarah, who looked like she had a preemptive eye roll locked and loaded.

"I think you know why we're here," I said. "Don't you, Sarah?"

"Nope," said Sarah, crossing her arms. "No clue. Maybe you want to go down Cid's stupid waterslide again or—"

"It's you," I said.

"Please. What are you even talking about?" said Sarah. "What's me? That's not even a—"

"This whole time I've been trying to figure out who the Saw is," I said. "But it was right there in plain sight: Saw. S-A-W. Sarah-Anne Wilkins. It's you."

Sarah looked like she was about to say something but she didn't.

"Hang on," said Cid. "Is Sam right? Is that true?"

"Yes," said Sarah.

"You tried to kill Hamstersaurus Rex?" said Cid. "But why?"

"BECAUSE!" shrieked Sarah. "Because our stupid dad and stepmom listened to you when you whined and whined and made our whole family uproot and move here for *no reason*! I had friends at our old school! People I cared about! They're all gone now."

"Oh, here we go again," said Cid. He turned to us and shook his head. "She's always so melodramatic."

"And you *always* get everything you want! It's completely unfair!" said Sarah. "But I knew there was one thing you wanted more than anything else: the mutant hamster you wouldn't shut up about; the whole point of coming to this stupid town; the reason you destroyed my life. So . . . I decided to take that thing from you."

"I'm guessing your dad gave you an advance-release Snuzzle, too, right, Sarah?" I said. "And you hacked it into an unstoppable killing machine."

"Wait," said Cid. "Sarah-Anne knows how to program computers?"

"Yes," said Sarah, waving her laptop, "which you might have actually noticed if you ever paid attention to anyone other than yourself."

"After that, you put the hacked Snuzzle on the shelf at Tenth Street Toys: a ticking time bomb," I said. "You even managed to erase the security footage of yourself doing it while Mr. Lomax was in the bathroom. But Hammie and I just happened to run into Gooboo a little early, before the virus could spread to any other Snuzzles. We're lucky we did or the little guy might not have survived."

Hammie growled.

"Look, it was nothing personal," said Sarah. "I didn't even know Hamstersaurus Rex! I just knew he lived in this town and I was mad at Cid and I—I did something rash. It was a mistake, okay?"

"Mad at me?" said Cid. "What did I do?"

Dylan groaned. "Man, are you self-centered."

"Yeah," said Beefer. "It's like, I know he's not even the real bad guy here, but I want to hit him so bad."

"Sarah," I said, "right now your virus is out of control. A deranged Snuzzle superorganism is heading through the woods toward the heart of Maple Bluffs. Once it gets to town, it will disrupt any electronics it even gets close to in its relentless quest to destroy Hamstersaurus Rex. People will get hurt."

"Look, I never thought it would get this far!" said Sarah. "I had no idea all the Snuzzles would learn to start working together like that! I just . . . I . . ."

"It doesn't matter what you thought," I said. "You're the only one who can stop it now."

Sarah was silent again.

"I also know that deep down, you're a good person," I said. "You're the one who left the mysterious note in my backpack: 'Don't trust him. He's a liar.' Remember? You were trying to warn me about Cid."

Sarah nodded. "I just hate the way he treats people. He's so manipulative."

"Uh, I prefer to think of it as 'persuasive,'" said Cid.

"Seriously, shut *up*, Cid," said Serena.

"Sarah, we need you to create a cure," said Martha. "A second virus can be transmitted wirelessly to all the infected Snuzzles to erase the first one."

Sarah took a deep breath. "Okay," she said. "I'll do it. But I'm going to need a clean Snuzzle."

"Cid's got one he never opened," I said. "Is there anything else you need?"

"Hmm," said Sarah. "A soda?"

We all looked at Cid.

"You heard her," said Beefer, cracking his knuckles.

"Wait . . . seriously?" said Cid.

Hammie Rex snarled.

Cid sighed. "What flavor?"

"Surprise me," said Sarah. And she pulled out her laptop and started to code.

CHAPTER 20

I COULD ALMOST FEEL the ground shake as it slowly rolled down the middle of Evergreen Street: a ten-foot-tall ball of Snuzzles, all clinging to one another and moving together as some sort of cuddly cybernetic superorganism.

"WOCATING PWIMAWY TAWGET!" boomed the adorable Snuzzle voices in unison. "WOCATING PWIMAWY TAWGET!"

A shocked Maple Bluffian stood on her lawn and attempted to take video of this bizarre sight but suddenly realized her phone had stopped working. She couldn't call the police if she wanted to. A car swerved to avoid hitting the Snuzzle-thing as it rolled past. A nearby streetlight flickered and then exploded in a shower of sparks.

"Yikes," said Dylan.

"MY NOSE IS FUZZY-WUZZY!" said the Snuzzle-thing. We watched through Beefer's binoculars from behind a row of recycling bins five blocks away.

"Let's go over the plan one more time," said Martha. "Just to be sure we're all on the same page." Martha held up Cid's Snuzzle, which Sarah had managed to hack in record time. "According to Sarah, the 'good' virus will take about three minutes to infect the bad Snuzzles. That means Bobbo here needs to be within range for that entire time."

"The box says these things can communicate wirelessly up to a hundred feet," said Dylan.

"Got it," I said. I took the Snuzzle from her. "What happens if I get out of range?"

"You'll have to start the upload over," said Martha. "Anyway, the Snuzzle collective's main objective is still to locate and destroy Hamster-saurus Rex. So we need to keep him out of sight and harm's way. That means hidden inside a PET-CATRAZ Pro™ far away from the action. Guarding him will be up to me and Drew."

"Who?" said Beefer.

"And tell me again how we stop the Snuzzle-thing from stomping on Bobbo's head before the 'good' virus can finish uploading?" said Dylan.

"You, Beefer, and Serena will create a distraction," I said. "With a little help from these three prehistoric fuzzballs!"

I held up Stompy, Chompy, and Hatshepsut. Hatshepsut was sniffing her own toes, while Stompy and Chompy were engaged in what could only be described as a head-butting contest. Hamstersaurus Rex whined in distress.

"Hammie, I know you're worried," I said. "You want your babies to be safe. But they can't be babies forever. You've seen what they're capable of."

"They kicked Gordon Renfro's butt!" said Serena.

"And destroyed a quarter of a million dollars in microscopes!" said Beefer.

"We need them to have a chance of stopping this Snuzzle-strosity once and for all," I said.

Hamstersaurus Rex stared at his pups for a long moment. Then he gave each one of them a slobbery smooch. It was tough to let go, but the little guy had made his peace with it. Or at least he was able to swallow his fear for the moment. I extended my finger to give him the world's tiniest high five. Then we put him inside the PETCATRAZ Pro™, locked it, and hid it in an empty recycling bin.

"Everybody ready?" I said.

"Ready!" said Dylan and Drew, accidentally in unison. They giggled. It was sickening . . . and kind of sweet. Dylan took Chompy.

"I'll take Stompy," said Serena. "She reminds me of a young me, but, like, as a hamster. With reptile feet."

“Ah, Hatshepsut,” said Beefer, picking the final hamster pup up. “Such a beautiful name. I wonder who might have chosen it. Yes, I truly, truly wonder.”

“Ahem. That would be me, Kiefer,” said Martha.

“Hatshepsut,” said Beefer. “Ancient Egyptian meaning ‘Foremost of the Noble Ladies’; Hatshepsut (1507–1458 BC) was the second historically confirmed female pharaoh. Citation needed.”

“Dude, did you just memorize, word for word, the whole Wiki page where you got that?” I said.

“Shut up, Sir Stinks-a-lot,” said Beefer. “And let me tell you about Hatshepsut: Builder. Edit. Hatshepsut was a prolific builder, commissioning hundreds of—”

“We don’t have time for this,” I said. “Ready, Bobbo?”

“FWIENDSHIP MEANS CAWING,” said the Snuzzle.

“It sure does,” I said. “Move out!”

Beefer and Serena broke left. Dylan and I broke right. We took Juniper Way, which runs parallel to Evergreen Street, in the general direction of the oncoming Snuzzle-thing.

“You know, Drew’s actually kind of a cool guy,” I said. “Not just anybody would agree to fight a ball of evil robots to save a hamster’s life.”

“Thanks,” said Dylan. “But truth be told, I’m still not a hundred percent sure he actually knows what’s going on. It’s very possible he still thinks this is all part of Model Interplanetary Council.”

We both laughed. It was good to be friends again.

“Okay,” said Dylan. “Let’s cut through here.”

We ducked through a backyard, back toward

Evergreen Street, and crouched behind a hedge. The Snuzzle-thing wasn't far now, only a few houses down.

"Ready, Chompy?" said Dylan.

The hamster pup growled.

"Now," I said.

Dylan held Chompy up and he let out his loudest hamster-dino roar. It sounded exactly like Hamstersaurus Rex! Down the street, the Snuzzle-thing paused.

". . . PWOBABLE VOCAL MATCH. PWIMAWY TAWGET DETECTED," it said. "DESTWOY!"

The Snuzzle-thing started rapidly rolling in our direction, flattening a birdbath with a horrendous crunch.

"Wish me luck!" said Dylan.

Then she took off back the way we had come. Meanwhile I ducked behind a tree as the Snuzzle-thing rolled past, following Dylan across the yard. It was within the hundred-foot range now.

Bobbo's big, adorable eyes rolled back in his head. "COMMENCING SECONDAWY VIWUS UPWOAD," said Bobbo. ". . . ONE PEWCENT COMPWETE."

I followed behind the rolling Snuzzle-thing as closely as I could while Dylan jogged ahead with Chompy. The hamster pup roared again.

". . . EWEVEN PEWCENT COMPWETE," said Bobbo.

Dylan sprinted across two more yards and leaped on top of a propane grill to scramble over a tall fence and into a third. A moment later, the Snuzzle-thing crashed through the fence behind her, sending planks and splinters flying. Dylan raced across the yard and hit another fence. But it was too tall to climb. She looked around and saw that there was nothing to help her get over it. Dylan jumped but she couldn't reach the top. The Snuzzle-thing crushed a lawn chair as it bore down on her and Chompy. Dylan jumped again and missed.

"I'm cornered!" yelled Dylan. "What do I do?"

"Show the Snuzzles it's not Hammie before that thing pancakes you!" I yelled.

"DESTWOY!" said the Snuzzle-thing.

Dylan held up Chompy, who snarled in defiance. The Snuzzle-thing froze.

". . . TAWGET MISIDENTIFICATION," said the Snuzzle-thing. "DISENGAGE AND WOCATE PWIMAWY TAWGET."

Just then another dino-hamster roar rang through the neighborhood: either Stompy or Hatshepsut. Perfect timing!

"PWIMAWY TAWGET DETECTED," said the Snuzzle-thing. It started to roll in the direction of the new sound.

So far the plan was working. By confusing the Snuzzle-thing we were buying ourselves the time we needed to upload the cure. I hoped it would be enough.

"FOWTY-FOUR PEWCENT COMPWETE," said Bobbo as I followed behind the Snuzzle-thing.

"Hurry up!" I said.

"I WUV YOU," said Bobbo.

"Hey! Yoo-hoo! Over here!" called Serena from across the street. She patted her shirt pocket. "I've got Hamstersaurus Rex with me, you big ol' ball of . . . *weird*!"

"PWIMAWY TAWGET WOCKED," said the Snuzzle-thing as it barreled toward Serena, crunching a no parking sign and a row of newly planted saplings. I scrambled after it, clutching Bobbo under my arm.

"SIXTY-SEVEN PEWCENT COMPWETE," said Bobbo.

But Stompy couldn't control herself. The thrill of the fight was too much. As Serena turned to run, Stompy burst out of her pocket like an alien from one of Beefer's horror movies.

"Aw, nuts!" cried Serena.

The hamster pup gave another mighty roar before charging right at the Snuzzle-thing. The Snuzzle-thing ignored her.

". . . TAWGET MISIDENTIFICATION," said the Snuzzle-thing. "DISENGAGE AND WOCATE

PWIMAWY TAWGET."

"SEVENTY-NINE PEWCENT COMPWETE," said Bobbo.

"WOCATING PWIMAW— WAWNING! WAWNING! VIWUS DETECTED," said the Snuzzle-thing. "WAWNING!"

The glowing red eyes of every Snuzzle turned toward me.

"Uh," I said.

"EIGHTY PEWCENT COMPWETE," said Bobbo.

"DESTWOY!" The Snuzzle-thing charged. I turned and ran.

"Guys! Somebody! Anybody!" I yelled. "Help!"

I raced down Evergreen Street with the Snuzzle-thing close on my heels. I kept looking over my shoulder to see if it was gaining on me. That's why I never saw the crack in the sidewalk. My foot caught on it and I tripped and fell. Bobbo went clattering across the pavement. The Snuzzle-thing kept coming. I covered my head and prepared to be crushed. Instead the Snuzzle-thing rolled past me toward Bobbo, lying on the ground ahead. One of the Snuzzles detached from the ball and approached.

"EIGHTY-ONE PEWCENT COMP—"

THWUMP! The evil Snuzzle delivered a robo-strength kick that sent Bobbo sailing through the air.

"OUT OF WANGE," I heard as Bobbo flew, "UPWOAD FAIWUUUUUWE . . ."

"No!" I said.

"Don't worry, Sam, I'm here to save you, yet again!" cried Beefer.

He stood on the corner across the street. Hatshepsut was hidden inside his cupped hands. She gave a powerful roar.

"Hear that?" said Beefer. "That's the sound of Martha Junior, aka Hamstersaurus Rex! And if you want this stupid gerbil you'll have to come and get him, dum-dum!"

"TAWGET WOCKED," said the Snuzzle-thing. "DESTWOY!"

The Snuzzle-thing started to roll toward him.

"Ninja run away fast maneuver GO!" cried Beefer, and he turned and ninja-ran-away-fast down Tenth Street.

I leaped to my feet and found Bobbo in a flower

bed, four yards down. The Snuzzle was dented but luckily still functional.

"BUTTEWFWY KISSES MAKE ME GIGGWE," said Bobbo as I picked him up.

I turned to see Martha racing toward me. She looked frantic.

"Sam!" she cried. "We have to stop Kiefer!"

"What?" I said. "Why?"

"He went down Tenth Street!"

My heart sank. "Toward Tenth Street Toys," I said. "Beefer's leading the Snuzzle-thing straight to a whole toy store full of reinforcements."

CHAPTER 21

"COMMENCING SECONDAWY VIWUS UPWOAD," said Bobbo. "ONE PEWCENT COMPWETE . . ."

Running as fast as I could, I'd finally caught up with the Snuzzle-thing as it hounded Beefer down Tenth Street. The streetlights nearby were going haywire. Car alarms gave strangely distorted wails. At Tip Top Electronics, a whole display window of TVs went all staticky. More panicked bystanders tried to call someone, anyone, only to find that their phones were useless.

"Beefer, stop!" I yelled as I got closer.

"Huh? No way! You stop!" he yelled back. "This

thing wants to smoosh me!"

"DESTWOY!" said the Snuzzle-thing.

"See?" yelled Beefer, who ran even faster. He was clearly terrified.

"You have to lead it in another direction!" I cried.

"What?" yelled Beefer. With all the noise, he was getting too far ahead to hear me.

"Keep it away from Tenth Street Toys!" I yelled.

"Tenth Street Toys!" yelled Beefer. "Got it!"

"No!" I yelled. "Away! Away from Tenth Street Toys!"

But it was too late. Hatshepsut gave another roar and Beefer made a beeline for the toy store. I could see Tenth Street Toys up ahead now. Mr. Lomax was out front sweeping the sidewalk with a push broom. Beefer nearly knocked him over as he dashed past, into the store.

"Hey, kid, didn't you see the sign?" said Mr. Lomax, squinting at Hatshepsut. "No weird, scaly hamsters!"

"Mr. Lomax, save yourself!" I called from down the street.

"Huh?" said Mr. Lomax. He blinked as he finally saw the Snuzzle-thing rolling down the street toward him.

"MY TOES AWE VEWY TICKWISH," thundered the many voices of the Snuzzle-thing.

"Well," said Mr. Lomax. "That's. Not. Good."

"THIWTEEN PEWCENT COMPWETE," said Bobbo.

"Aaaaaagh!" screamed Beefer as he burst back out of the store with Hatshepsut, nearly knocking Mr. Lomax over a second time. "Why did you tell me to go in there, Sam? It's an ambush!"

"DESTWOY!" said the Snuzzle-thing as it swerved to follow Beefer, flattening several parking meters in the process.

"What in the world is going on?" said Mr. Lomax.

"It's the Cutepocalypse!" I said as I shoved him out of the way an instant before his display window shattered behind him.

"DESTWOY! . . . DESTWOY! . . . DESTWOY! . . ."

Two hundred more Snuzzles—every single one that Mr. Lomax had in stock—had now been

infected. They marched out of the broken window and through the door of Tenth Street Toys. The Snuzzles swarmed toward the Snuzzle-thing, which absorbed them into the collective. I watched in horror as the Snuzzle-thing grew, and grew, and grew. It stood twenty feet tall now. No longer a lumpy ball—it had arms, legs, and even big bat-like ears. The whole thing had assumed the rough shape of a colossal Snuzzle.

"WADICAL, BWO," bellowed the many voices of the Snuzzle-thing, which sent Mr. Lomax and every other remaining bystander fleeing in terror.

"Save me!" cried Beefer as he ran down the street and dove behind a dumpster.

"DESTWOY!" said the Snuzzle-thing as it strode after him, leaving cracks in the pavement with each step.

"TWENTY-ONE PEWCENT COMPWETE," said Bobbo.

SCREEECH! A Maple Bluffs police cruiser squealed to a halt between Beefer and the Snuzzle-thing. Even without phones, someone must have finally gotten word to the cops. Two officers leaped out of the car.

One of them held up a loud-speaker. "Uh, please freeze," he said in a quavery voice, "and put your—I guess they're

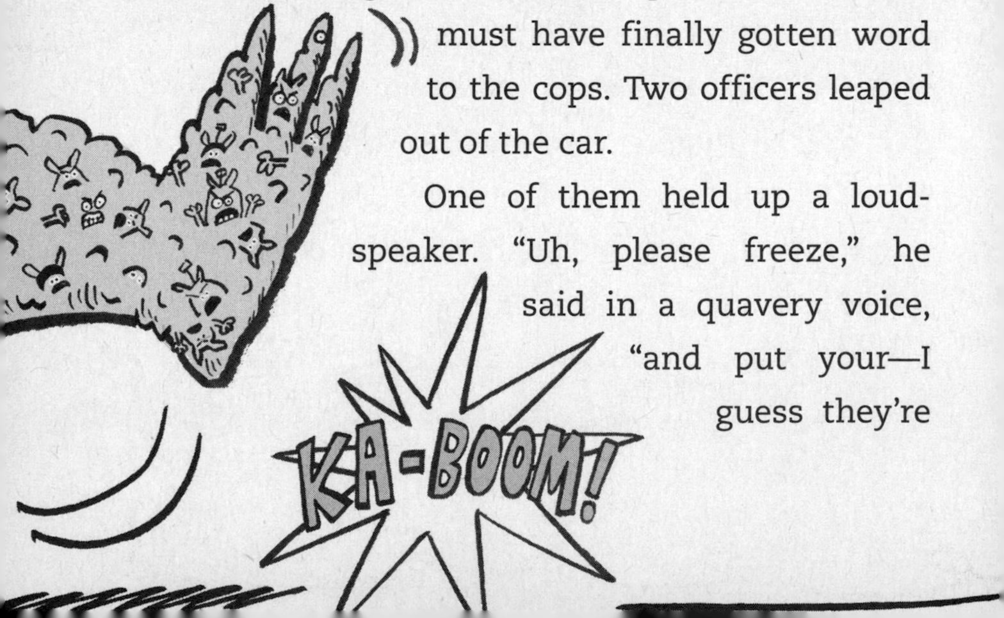

KA-BOOM!

hands—up. If that's okay with you?"

"NEUTWAWIZE SECONDAWY TAWGET," said the Snuzzle-thing. It kicked the police cruiser with a massive foot, sending the vehicle spinning sideways into a nearby telephone pole. At this, both the officers lost their nerve and ran for their lives. I couldn't exactly blame them: they probably didn't cover arresting two-story toy monsters at the academy.

But it meant stopping the Snuzzle-thing was all up to us now.

"TWENTY-SEVEN PEWCENT COMPWETE," said Bobbo.

With one arm the Snuzzle-thing flung the dumpster aside, to reveal Beefer cowering behind it, still cradling Hatshepsut in his hands.

"No!" I said.

"My only regret was not seeing *Wolfsplosion IV* in theaters," whimpered Beefer.

"PWIMAWY TAWGET

WOCKED!" said the Snuzzle-thing as it raised its other fist high above its head. "DESTW—"

From behind me there came a roar as loud as a thunderclap. It was no hamster pup this time, but the unmistakable battle cry of Hamstersaurus Rex. I turned to see the others running toward me down the street: Serena, Dylan, Martha, and Drew, who clutched the PETCATRAZ Pro™ under his arm. Inside was Hammie Rex.

"Sorry, Sam," said Martha. "I thought this might be our only hope to draw the Snuzzle-thing away! But we're too late!"

"Just don't let it get Hammie Rex!" I called back.

"TAWGET MISIDENTIFCATION," said the Snuzzle-thing as it turned to face Hamstersaurus Rex. "ENGAGING PWIMA— WAWNING! WAWNING! VIWUS DETECTED!"

The Snuzzle-thing spun toward me. I dove out of the way as its giant fist slammed into the ground where I'd been standing, cratering the asphalt.

"THIWTY-THWEE PEWCENT COMPWETE," said Bobbo, who I'd somehow still managed to hold on to.

I scrambled to my feet. "Take this!" I said, tossing Bobbo to Dylan. Hamstersaurus Rex let out another roar. I guess the little guy was trying to warn me, because a split second later a flying trash can—hurled by the Snuzzle-thing—knocked me off my feet.

After that, everything went dark.

I don't know how much time passed before I felt something tickling my fingers. I sat up to see that Hamstersaurus Rex was licking my hand. But how was he licking my hand? Wasn't he locked inside a cage? I turned to see the PETCATRAZ Pro™ lying on the sidewalk nearby. I blinked. Two of the titanium bars had been bent. Hamstersaurus Rex had done the impossible: he had escaped from the toughest small rodent cage on the market! I reached over to scratch him and realized I had a splitting headache.

My mind was cloudy but it was starting to clear. "Wait . . . the Snuzzle-thing," I said, remembering. "We have to stop the Snuzzle-thing!"

Hammie growled.

"We still have one trick left," I said. I unzipped

my backpack and pulled out two canisters: one labeled “PaleoGro,” the other labeled “Huginex-G.” I’d swiped them on our way out of the underground lab.

“According to Gordon Renfro, a combined dose of these two will make you ‘combat ready,’” I said. “Whatever that’s supposed to mean.”

I poured the viscous blue Huginex-G into the powdery green PaleoGro, put the lid back on, and then shook the concoction. I opened it again to see I’d mixed up a bright teal sludge cocktail.

“Okay,” I said. “Down the hatch.”

I upended the canister into Hamstersaurus Rex’s mouth. He slurped down the stuff until there was none left, and then he licked his chops.

“. . . Well?”

Hamstersaurus Rex gave a little hiccup. And then he started to grow and . . . change. His legs swelled with muscles and his tail elongated. Still he grew, as his round hamster face stretched into a large snout with rows of pointy teeth. Still he grew, as razor-sharp talons sprouted from his toes and all his fur fell out in clumps.

The transformation was complete: the little guy stood fifteen feet high and forty feet long from his nose to his tail. There was no trace of hamster left in him. He had become a full-fledged Tyrannosaurus rex.

"Whoa," I said.

Hammie cocked his head to stare at me with a yellow eye. I suddenly wondered if he still remembered that I was his friend and not a snack. He opened his jaws wide to reveal his glistening fangs and . . . he gave me a slobbery lick—only now his tongue was as big as my head!

"Ready to save the day?" I said.

Hamstersaurus Rex grunted and lowered his head and I swung a leg over his neck.

"Then let's go!" I said.

Hammie rose and started to run—with me riding on his back!

We caught up to the Snuzzle-thing on the corner of Walnut Street and Tenth. With a mighty swipe, it flipped over a car and sent it rolling into a nearby yard. It was still looking for Bobbo.

"Sam!" whispered Martha, who was hiding

behind a mailbox. "Why are you riding on a—is that—what?"

"I know!" I said. "Just go with it!"

The Snuzzle-thing tore the roof off a toolshed to reveal Dylan and Bobbo hiding inside. Dylan gasped.

"DESTWOY," said the Snuzzle-thing.

Hammie lowered his T. rex head like a battering ram and charged. He hit the Snuzzle-thing squarely in the back, staggering it. Broken Snuzzles flew everywhere.

Dylan sprinted out of the shed.

"SIXTY-THWEE PEWCENT COMPWETE," said Bobbo.

The Snuzzle-thing spun and swung its fist at Hammie, catching him with a heavy blow to the nose. Hammie spun back and bit into its arm, tearing out dozens of Snuzzles. He chomped at the Snuzzle-thing again and again.

"SEVENTY-SEVEN PEWCENT COMPWETE."

Hamstersaurus Rex had bowled the Snuzzle-thing over now, and he was clawing at it with his hind legs as he still crunched Snuzzles between his teeth. The Snuzzle-thing flailed wildly.

"EIGHTY-FIVE PEWCENT COMPWETE."

The Snuzzle-thing had lost its giant Snuzzle shape now. It had split into two amorphous balls and each of them slammed into Hamstersaurus Rex, pummeling him from two sides. He stumbled and then whipped his tail into one while kicking at another. More shattered Snuzzles went flying.

"NINETY-NINE PEWCENT COMPWETE."

The Snuzzle-thing had separated out into its constituent Snuzzles now. They all seemed to be fleeing in separate directions from the wrath of Hamstersaurus Rex, who was grinding them into the pavement and popping them between his teeth.

"UPWOAD COMPWETE," said Bobbo.

Suddenly, all the fleeing Snuzzles froze. Their eyes no longer glowed red. There was a moment of silence.

". . . HEWWO, FWIEND," said one.

"CAN I GIVE YOU A WITTWE SMOOCH?" asked another.

"CEWTAINWY," said a third.

They kissed. The newly benign Snuzzles all

started toddling in random directions and chatting adorably with one another.

Hamstersaurus Rex lurched beneath me.

"Whoa there," I said. "Easy, boy."

"Hey, Sam, do you know you're, like, on top of a dinosaur?" called Beefer from down the street, carrying Hatshepsut.

"Oh, am I?" I said. "That's weird."

Hammie bucked again and then he started to shrink. The effects of the Huginex-G and the PaleoGro were beginning to wear off. A few seconds later, the little guy had completely reverted to his normal (?) dino-hamster form.

Drew and Serena emerged from their hiding place in a nearby carport carrying Stompy and Chompy. Hammie snuggled each of his pups, who climbed all over him, still pretty hopped up from the epic fight against evil.

"It feels good to be reunited with the ones you love, huh?" I said.

"Mmm, it sure does," said Serena, cuddling her smartphone, which was now fully functional once again.

“We may not have won Best Delegation at Model Interplanetary Council,” said Martha, “but we did save the town from an uprising of deranged robots. Any reasonable college admissions board will have to take that into consideration. Right?”

“Guys, that was intense!” said Drew, whose eyes looked like they might bug out of his head. “Those Snuzzles were like, ‘’Sup!’ and then Hamstersaurus Rex was like, ‘’SUP!’ and then Dylan was like—”

“Yep! This is just part of being friends with Sam Gibbs,” said Dylan, throwing an arm around my shoulder. “And Hamstersaurus Rex.”

“You’ll get used to it,” I said to Drew.

Drew gave me a double thumbs-up.

Beefer nudged me. “Dude,” he whispered, “who is that guy?”

CHAPTER 22

"BOY, IT SURE feels strange to be back here," said my mom as she pulled into the parking lot. Her voice was muffled thanks to the industrial-grade dust mask she wore to keep her allergies under control. She checked herself out in the rearview. "Sam, does this mask look weird?"

It did.

"Nope," I said. "It's actually very stylish and cool. I'm sure once the other moms see you, they're all going to want one."

"Well, I thought it was important to be here today," said my mom. "But don't worry, I won't hover. I'm sure you want to hang out with all your little friends. I know you're practically a seventh grader now, Bunnybutt."

"Thanks, Mom," I said. "I'll catch you inside."

She gave me a kiss on the head and I grabbed my backpack and hopped out of the car.

As I crossed the parking lot, I unzipped my bag to see Stompy, Chompy, and Hatshepsut wrestling inside. Meanwhile, Hamstersaurus Rex, exhausted, stared blankly into the middle distance, whle Cartimandua snoozed.

"Guys," I said, "I want you all to be on your best behavior because . . . Aw, who am I kidding? We all know that's not going to happen. Just try not to burn the place down, okay?"

Hammie poked his head out, saw where we were, and gave a warning snarl.

"I know, dude. It gives me the creeps, too," I said. "But you have to remember: it's not Smiles-Corp anymore."

Not far away, I spotted Martha walking toward the entrance.

"Hey, Martha!" I said. "Glad you could make it!"

"Oh, hello, Sam!" said Martha. "Or should I say: *Doh meefa, xeesotee! Zlorrrrk.*"

I stared at her.

"I'm joking!" she said. "That's the traditional greeting of Zoblorg VII. Remember?"

I stared at her.

"Ugh," she said. "I honestly wish someone would explain the purpose of jokes, because I still don't get it. Anyway, how's your summer been?"

"Pretty boring," I said. "I spent most of it doing odd jobs for Old Man Ohlman: rearranging his weather vanes; painting his leaves; de-ghosting his closets, et cetera. I think I clocked, like, two hundred hours."

"Really?" she said. "Why?"

"I'm still trying to pay back the money I owe Tenth Street Toys," I said.

"But you saved Mr. Lomax's life!" said Martha.

"I know, I know," I said, "that's why he gave me an extension. I have until Labor Day and at this point I only owe him $11.21. Feels good to be in the home stretch."

Martha and I joined a line of people queuing

up to get inside Building Seven—formerly the SmilesCorp Genetic Research and Development Lab. A banner that read "Grand Opening" hung across the door.

"Hi, guys!" Dylan bounded over and joined us.

"Hey, Dylan," I said. "How was disc golf camp?"

"Amazing," said Dylan. "Alonso 'The Wrist' Chapman really helped me add some distance to my hyzer throw and he sold my dad a used station wagon! It was a win-win."

"Very cool," I said.

Drew joined us, carrying two ice cream cones. He handed one to Dylan.

"Howdy," said Drew.

Martha and I looked at each other.

"Howdy?" I said. "Not ''Sup'?"

"I'm just trying something new," said Drew with a shrug. "Don't box me in. I'm a complex, three-dimensional person with hopes and dreams. For example, did you know I—"

"What do you mean Michael Perkins isn't on the VIP list?" someone up ahead yelled.

I looked at the front of the line to see Beefer

arguing with the ticket-taker. Michael Perkins, his feathery boakeet, was coiled around his shoulders.

"I'm sorry, sir," said the woman, looking at her clipboard, "but I don't see that name here."

"Well, check again!" said Beefer. "Ever seen Epic Ninja 360-Degree Fail? That's me! As a celebrity I think I ought to be able to get a plus-one to this thing!"

I intervened, and after a bit of negotiation, we all agreed that for a mutant snake, half-price admission was fair. The rest of us *were* on the list, which I have to admit was pretty cool.

Inside, I almost couldn't believe my eyes. Building Seven looked totally different now. No longer dark and filled with strange lab equipment, it was now bright and friendly, divided up into spacious animal enclosures. Nearby, tourists snapped pictures of the duck with fur as it paddled around a realistic, simulated pond. Another enclosure held a woodland habitat with a sign that read: "Behold the Mighty Squirrel Kong!" Inside sat a grumpy-looking, regular-sized squirrel. A third enclosure, full of tall climbing trees and rope ladders, held the Chameleonkey.

"Mom, I don't see *anything*," said a disappointed kid, pressed up against the glass.

I spotted Serena over by the snack table. She was interviewing Coach Weekes.

". . . You know, if Hamstersaurus Rex had never eaten my Dinoblast Powerpacker, none of this would have ever happened," said Coach Weekes. "So in a way, if you think about it, I'm the real hero."

"Uh-huh," said Serena.

I waved to her and she cut her interview with Coach Weekes short.

"Hi, Serena Sandoval, legitimate journalist for my own blog," she said, pointing the microphone in my direction now. "Sam Gibbs, how does it feel to attend the grand opening of the Maple Bluffs Sanctuary for Atypical Animals?"

"Great!" I said. "For better or worse, our town has become known for mutant hybrids. Why not lean into it and make it a tourist attraction? Plus, it gives us something to do with all the weird critters."

"Weird critters indeed," said Serena, "and none weirder than Hamstersaurus Rex. Isn't that right?"

Hammie hopped out of my bag and gave a little bow. He was honored at the distinction.

"Well, I definitely think his kids are going to give him a run for his money in the weird department," I said. I peeked into my bag and saw that the only hamster left was a sleeping Cartimandua. "Wait, where are his kids?"

Hammie gave a panicked yelp and dashed off through the crowd to find them.

"Care to comment on the huge, anonymous donation to purchase the campus from Pappy's Beeswax of Maine and convert it into this facility?" said Serena.

"I have a theory on who the donor is," I said. "But I'm sure they'd prefer to remain anonymous."

Across the room, I saw Sarah Wilkins. Instead of scowling or eye rolling, she was eating hors d'oeuvres and chatting with some kids her age, laughing a little. For once, she'd been able to pester her dad into doing something that she wanted: creating the Maple Bluffs Sanctuary for Atypical Animals.

Suddenly, Cid Wilkins slid into my field of vision.

"Sam Dunk!" said Cid. "Long time no see, buddy. Hey, I've got this new indoor hang glider course at my house. No big deal. You should really

drop by and check it out sometime!"

"Thanks for the offer," I said. "I think I'm good, Cid."

"Speaking of offers," said Cid, "I'm glad I completely coincidentally ran into you at this little shindig because I am prepared to make you a substantial cash offer to purchase Hamstersaurus Rex—"

"Sorry, I've got to go, Cid," I said. "My friends are waiting."

I found Martha, Beefer, Dylan, and Drew standing by a wooded enclosure with several "DANGER!" and "KEEP BACK!" signs posted on it. It held the Grizzly Hare, a fearsome beast that was part hare, part grizzly bear.

"What are we looking at?" I said.

"That," said Dylan. She pointed.

Inside the enclosure, the Grizzly Hare stalked back and forth, growling and baring its fangs. Suddenly, a tiny shape popped out from a hollow log and blew a raspberry at the beast: it was Hatshepsut! The Grizzly Hare snarled, but Hatshepsut ducked back inside the log just in time to avoid getting chomped. In the meantime, Stompy crept out from under a rock and kicked an acorn at the Grizzly Hare. The Grizzly Hare ran at her but she dove back into her hiding place. While all of this was happening, Chompy was gobbling down everything in the Grizzly Hare's food dish.

"Perhaps we should intervene?" said Martha.

She pointed to Hamstersaurus Rex, who stood at the edge of the enclosure. The little guy looked like he was about to hyperventilate.

"Nah, I think they're okay," I said. "Maybe taunting deadly mutant beasts is just, you know, part of growing up?"

"If you say so," said Martha.

Cartimandua snuggled

up beside Hammie. (I hadn't even realized she'd escaped from my bag. Maybe Hamstersaurus Rex wasn't the only one the pups got their adventurous streak from?) Hammie took a deep breath, and the two of them watched their babies play along with the rest of us.

Somehow it felt like the end of an era for Hamstersaurus Rex. They say he was a giant among rodents, a folk hero for all time, even the pride of Mr. Copeland's sixth-grade class. To me, he was a friend. And I'm happy to say, one of many.

TOM O'DONNELL has written for *The New Yorker*, *McSweeney's*, and the television shows *Jeff & Some Aliens*, *TripTank*, *Right Now Kapow*, and *Billy on the Street*. His comic strips have been featured in *The New York Press* and *The Village Voice*. He lives with his wife and family in Brooklyn, New York. Read more at www.tomisokay.com.

TIM MILLER is the author-illustrator of *Moo Moo in a Tutu* and *What's Cooking, Moo Moo?* and the illustrator of the picture books *Snappsy the Alligator (Did Not Ask to Be in This Book!)*, *Snappsy the Alligator and His Best Friend Forever! (Probably)*, and *Margarash*. He lives in New Jersey with his wife and their cats. You can visit Tim online at www.timmillerillustration.com.

YOU MAY ALSO LIKE

HARPER

An Imprint of HarperCollins*Publishers*

WWW.HARPERCOLLINSCHILDRENS.COM